WATER
MUSIC

I am proud of what I have achieved during my years racing superbikes. Now my ambition is to use my racing talents on four wheels. Over the last 12 months I have had a lot of time for reflection and can feel my focus moving on to the future. On January 19, 2002, I'll be 36 years of age, yet I feel I am as strong and fast as ever. When Michael Schumacher set a new milestone for Formula One victories in 2001, Ferrari team manager Jean Todt was asked how long he thought Schumacher could race at the top of the sport. He replied, "It doesn't matter how old he gets, it's what's inside that counts."

Inside me there still beats the heart of a champion. I can sit back on my New Zealand Order of Merit, all my Sportsman of the Year awards, my 13 WSB wins, 42 seconds, 32 thirds, and the three consecutive Suzuka 8-Hour victories, and say I had a successful career. However, I can't tell anyone that finishing second in the title twice, and third four times felt really great, or completely satisfied me. At the time I was happy with those performances because I honestly couldn't see how I could have tried any harder. But mostly I felt as beat as Scott Russell did at the Suzuka 8-Hour in 1994. Getting beat only makes me all the more determined to win the next race.

Whatever happens in my future racing career, it's not over yet.

Home Is Where Your Dildo Is

B asher and Alex lived in a terraced flat on the top of a windy hill in Brighton. The buildings were white, tall and narrow, with dark doors and steps, and window frames that stretched from floor to ceiling. Without embellishments by the occupants, they would look like a row of very serious, teetering seagulls.

The occupants, however, had embellished aplenty. Every third or fourth flat had some kind of banner or flag or poster displaying various affiliations, or else could not be seen because there were too many plants on the outside sill. Basher's flat, which was on the second floor, was next to one that had a massive rainbow Pride blanket pinned up instead of a curtain, and below one that had an Algerian flag and a 'SAVE THE NHS' poster.

Claire huffed and puffed and coughed up a mere two flights of stairs so much that she had to rest once she got to the door, and Alex glanced at her with some alarm. When they got inside, Basher hurried to the toilet and produced a sparkly purple pill organizer. The days of the week were, indeed, marked by letters formed from small but impressively detailed model penises. They were of many shapes, colours and sizes.

'Off for a stare, Uncle Bash?' Alex asked. 'I'll put the kettle on anyway.'

'Yes. Be all right if I can get a nap in, I think,' he said. He yawned by way of proof, and vanished into his bedroom.

Alex gave Sophie and Claire the short tour. The living room faced the street, and was large enough to hold a corner sofa in front of a coffee table and TV, *and* a table and chairs for dinnertime. There were books everywhere, mostly with charity shop stickers still on them, which Claire attributed to Basher. The kitchen was stuck onto one side of the living room, and the toilet – which was covered from floor to ceiling in small white square tiles, and made Claire feel vaguely like she was inside a tooth – was behind the living room and at the top of a narrow hallway; Basher's bedroom door was at the other end, with a third in between. They were not allowed in Basher's room, not even a brief look for completeness. Claire found this suspicious. What could he have to hide? Evidence that he had murdered his partner, perchance?

Claire caught herself there. It was very unlikely he had, for instance, a year-old body in there. It would smell. Also, if she did really think Basher was a potential murderer, then it was very silly of her to have come here.

It was a nice flat, even though the enormously high ceilings were festooned in cobwebs that neither permanent occupant had the motivation to hoick down. Claire was a card-carrying member of Generation Rent, and that card was an overdrawn one. She swallowed some resentment.

Alex opened the third door with a saved-the-best-till-last flourish. The first thing at Claire's direct eye level was a shelf of bright purple dildos in different shapes.

'Ohmigod. I mean, I guess your decorating has a clear *theme*...' said Sophie, snorting with laughter.

'Eh, they're for a thing,' said Alex, pathologically unembarrassed. 'Just not sure what, yet. A friend works making them, and there was a flaw in the curing of these or something. They're too wobbly. So she gave them to me. I thought maybe, like, unicorn horns, but dicks?' They chucked a distinctly thick dildo at Claire, who caught it.

'*Way* too on-the-nose,' said Claire. She flicked it and it *boinged*.

'Yeah, you're right,' said Alex. 'Someone would definitely buy that, though, is the thing...'

'What about mounting them on, like, a plaque, with "Home Is Where Your Dildo Is" painted on it?' pitched Sophie.

Alex was delighted by this suggestion. 'They *do* say that, don't they?'

The rest of Alex's room was as messy as the inside of their pockets undoubtedly were. There was what Claire assumed was a bed, buried under a heap of clothes. There was also a work desk that appeared to be doing similar double duty as a wardrobe.

Apart from that, every available surface was covered with *stuff*. Embroidery thread, fabric, empty bottles, plant pots, paint pots, interesting rocks, marbles, two halves of different picture frames stuck together, a bit of modelling foam half sanded into the shape of something else, the ammunition for a hot-glue gun but without a glue gun in sight, many jars of sequins and buttons. It was a very eclectic assault on the senses.

'So, yes, this is *my* room, and as you can see it is amazing. Don't worry, I definitely know where everything is. Just don't... don't walk around too much.'

Claire looked down and was unable to see carpet.

'What's this all for?' asked Sophie, who was unburdened by physical feet and was having a good nose around.

'I make kitschy *stuff* to sell online,' said Alex. They sat down on the edge of their bed. 'It's going... well, not amazingly, if we're honest. Also,' they added, after a pause, 'I'm still in the "making friends" stage here, really. Brighton is cool, but I've not been living here long. My school friends are all at uni. I'm actually – like, I sell things I make, and Mum sends me money, but I work at the library. Bash's council connections, I guess.'

It was the first time Claire had heard them say anything remotely age-appropriate. Sophie looked shocked as well. She went and sat next to Alex.

'I know who I am,' Alex added, 'but it's much harder to figure out what I want to *do*. Or how to do it.'

'I don't think most people ever know how to do anything really,' said Sophie. 'The trick about life – speaking as an outside observer – is realizing that everyone is making it up as they go, all the time. Even David Attenborough and people like that.'

'Hmm.' Alex hefted a dildo thoughtfully in one hand. 'What did you want to be when you grew up?'

'Famous,' said Sophie. 'On the bright side, I suppose I sort of was, for a bit.'

'That's a very bleak sort of bright side.'

'You learn to take wins where you can get 'em.'

Claire felt as if she was eavesdropping, even though she was an integral part of the conversation. 'That's great, though,' she said, to cover her embarrassment. 'Libraries are fucking awesome.'

They left Alex to change their clothes, and Claire went for a wee in the big tooth-room. The toilet had long ago been established as a restricted zone where Soph could not follow, along with whenever Claire had a man over, or whenever she went to the doctor.

Claire realized she was still holding the dildo, which was surprisingly weighty, and put it on the side of the bath. An ancient kettle shuddered and roared like some latter-day species of sex toy – a terrifying, steam-powered nineteenth-century one, loud enough that Claire could hear it all this way from the kitchen. Hysterical paroxysms for women: satisfaction guaranteed.

Chance, considered Claire, with some detachment, *would be a fine bloody thing*, although truthfully she had always regarded the sex part of relationships with apathy at best. This was another source of annoyance to Sophie, who regarded it as 'a massive fucking waste' and, when they were arguing, cited it as yet another reason it was monstrously unfair that she was the dead one.

For reasons she could not entirely explain to herself or Sophie, who thought it was very funny, Claire stowed the wibbly dildo in her rucksack. It was one of those ubiquitous Vans rucksacks with the white-and-black chequered front, but because she had had it since school, the white squares were almost grey. Some of them had long ago been coloured in with different highlighter pens or biro.

In the kitchen, the kettle had finished boiling, but whichever Wellington-Forge had turned it on had vanished back to their room. Claire decided to be a good house-guest and make the tea herself.

Sophie noticed her hesitating with the spoon. 'Hmm. Well, Bash is a splash of milk, no sugar – that's obvious. Heaven forbid he should allow himself to enjoy anything. But there *is* sugar next to the tea caddy, so that means…?'

'Alex probably takes some.'

'Right!'

'You don't have to be so patronizing about it.'

Claire took her shoes off and crept stealthily down the hall to Basher's room. She hesitated, then pushed an ear towards the door. She could hear a faint, gentle snore every few seconds. She thought again about the peach fuzziness of his stubble.

Sophie's face hove into her view from the side, with glacial slowness and a similar accompanying blast of frigid air. Her eyes were narrowed. 'And what exactly the fuck are you doing now?' she hissed. 'Ohmigod. Please. No. Stop!'

In the end Claire put the tea down in front of Basher's door and hurried off, as Soph carried on berating her.

'You're worse than those proper weirdos who go on relationship subreddits.'

'Shut up.'

'"I [30F] am a big creepy loser who listens to my new friend [28M] breathing through the door, how can I take things to the next level?"'

'I know.'

'If you do that again, I swear I'll find a way to tell him. I thought you didn't even like Basher,' said Sophie.

'I don't, he's annoying. What kind of real person casually drops Shakespeare quotes into everyday conversation? Nobody. It's something you have to try, like, really hard to do.'

'And yet you fancy him?'

'I dunno. A bit? Maybe?'

'Probably because he's the only man you've spent more than an hour with in one go for, like, a whole year. You can't actually fancy someone you don't like.'

'That is *one hundred per cent* untrue – of course you can.'

'Okay, yeah, but you can't form a proper long-term relationship with someone you don't like.'

'A lifetime of watching reruns of sitcoms from the noughties has taught me that heterosexual couples aren't s'posed to like each other or have anything in common,' said Claire. 'It's probably a Pavlovian response, if anything.'

'Ohmigod. As arguments for the Defence go, "I was trained to fancy people I don't like by Ross from *Friends*" is pretty weak,' Soph replied, raising an eyebrow. 'Anyway I *do* like him, and Alex, and if you ruin this by being creepy, I'll never speak to you again.'

'I *know*, I know, fuck off, I won't.'

But Claire was appropriately shamed. She didn't want to ruin any burgeoning friendships, because those can be hard to come by, when you have the habit of occasionally saying things to thin air; and they become mostly non-existent when you disclose that your actual job is being a medium. Or, rather, the people who did want to be Claire's friend at that point were all really intense and offputting, and did stuff like trying to cultivate psychic connections with ravens, while Claire did, at a basic level, view herself and Sophie as pretty normal. Like, apart from the obvious.

The rest of their trip back through the New Forest had gone well. Basher and Alex had shared stories about Nana, catharting quite merrily. Claire had been the intermediary in a long conversation between Soph and Alex about embroidery, which Sophie claimed to find very interesting. The bonus was that Claire relaying questions about specific colour choices or stitches that Alex was doing – but which Claire, in the front seat, couldn't be seeing herself – seemed to erase any remaining doubts Alex had about Sophie's existence, and even, she hoped, a couple of Basher's.

And when they got on the motorway proper, Basher had put on the radio and 'Mr Brightside' was playing, so he and Claire ended up sing-yelling it in a pretty good imitation of the pissed-up top table at every wedding that either of them had ever been to in their adult lives. Alex filmed it, to make fun of them on social media later. It had all been quite nice.

'Just don't ruin this by being all weird, you big weirdo,' said Sophie now. Her tone wasn't totally unkind. 'I wonder when we'll get to meet this Sami person,' she added. 'It's, like, we're really making progress now, so I don't want to stop.'

'Living people need to sleep, though, Soph.'

'I *know*. It's just so fucking boring. You have no idea how bad it is having to hang around doing *nothing*.'

Claire wasn't sure what Sophie did when Claire was unconscious. She knew that Sophie didn't disappear, but could walk a little way from her, and did. But sometimes she didn't. Claire would wake in the night and see the faintly luminous outline of a figure in the corner of the room, or by the door. At this point it would take a lot to make her afraid of the dark.

'I leave the TV on for you, you're fine. It's like leaving a dog home alone, but way less cute and likeable.'

'*Ohmigod*. Such a bitch.'

Claire threw a cushion through Soph in a lazy, automatic way, and then remembered they weren't her cushions and picked it up again.

Alex, who had a peculiar knack for bursting into rooms at the most convenient time, came back in with their blue hair in a messy bun on top of their head, wearing yellow jeans and a crisp white shirt with rolled-up sleeves. They looked a bit like an iced-gem biscuit, but, like, were totally pulling it off.

Alex was not only confident enough to wear all these things, but also clearly knew that confidence was the best way to look good doing it. They were also physically gifted – while only a little taller than Claire and Soph, their shoulders, hips and feet were all perfectly balanced against one another, and Alex had the same bone structure as the rest of their family. It's usually an insincere compliment to say that someone would look good wearing anything, but in Alex's case it was probably true. Claire was quite jealous, and said so out loud.

'Me, too,' added Sophie. 'You should dress Claire, Alex. Her wardrobe hasn't expanded much over the last – what – three years?'

'I can't afford to expand fuck all,' said Claire, looking down at the same grey jeans and jumper that she'd worn to arrive at – and depart – the Wellington-Forges.

'That doesn't have to be true,' said Alex. 'I get most of my clothes from charity shops.'

Claire could not fathom this attitude. She didn't approve of people having loads of money, but she also thought rather perversely that if your family *did* have money, and several houses, you could at least have the decency to behave like it. Alex didn't have to pay rent, was still financially supported by their parents and could clearly afford to shop at, for example, Zara and John Lewis, but appeared to be cosplaying at having a stretched budget; Claire could not really afford her rent *or* to buy new clothes. Surely Alex could subsidize one of them for her? Even a new pair of shoes? It seemed only fair. Then Claire would have new shoes, and Alex would have a reason for buying second-hand ones. Everyone wins.

She sighed heavily. She remembered being nineteen. Alex was very sincere, and burning with confidence and righteousness like a bin fire at a student protest, but they clearly weren't an idiot.

'You all right?' asked Alex. They looked concerned; they had the same lively grey eyes as Basher and Nana, so it almost seemed like the three of them were a little family unto themselves.

'Yeah,' replied Claire. 'I'm all right. Just sometimes how fucking weird this all is sort of, like, hits me, you know? And it's not even my family, so I dunno how you're coping.'

'I'm okay,' said Alex. They hauled one of the windows open and started smoking. They actually looked quite precarious, because it was a sash window that opened directly upwards and had a low sill and no safety railing. 'I think the murder thing is distracting me from Nana dying, and Nana dying is distracting me from the murder thing. They've cancelled each other out, so I'm basically normal.'

'Better brace for whenever one of them gets resolved,' said Sophie. She went to sit on Alex's feet, like she did with Claire. She seemed to be enjoying making her presence felt by people who sort of knew she was there, and what was happening when she did it.

Alex pulled their socks off. They nodded and agreed that they would most likely be in an absolute state after the funeral, but they weren't thinking about that now. 'I mean,' they said, 'it's odd to realize that even without the murder thing, I don't think that, as a family, we really like each other very much.'

'Yeah but that's true of a lot of families. Most, probably,' said Claire, thinking about how often she spoke to her own parents, which was: not often. Her dad lived in Norwich with a nice woman who had strong opinions about rooms needing to have a feature wall in a pattern or a bright colour, and he called her on Christmas, birthdays and other special occasions. Her mum still lived in London and worked in a sensible bookshop, and they avoided one another so that the subject of Claire's profession never had to come up in conversation.

She shared this with Alex. 'It's, like, I was in therapy for so long, over saying Sophie existed. They almost had me convinced that she didn't. And now, doing what I do... It's like all of it was a waste of time and money, and they might as well not have spent it, and maybe Mum and Dad would have stayed together.'

'I think it's like, to her, if you tried hard enough, you'd be normal,' said Soph. 'But from our point of view, there's not actually anything wrong with you.'

Alex said 'Ooof' with some solemnity. 'With us,' they went on, 'it felt like Nana was the one thing that kept us all together. She was the one who loved us and wanted to know what we were all up to, and wanted us to be together and talk to each other. And she wanted to know everything, and try everything. I dunno how our family ever produced her. She very nearly got me to shave her eyebrows like mine, once. Now that she's gone, I don't know what else there is for the family. Except that house.'

'Was last year what made you come and move down here?' Sophie asked.

'Yeah,' said Alex. 'I love Mum, and Dad even, because, you know: he's my dad. But it's like, at what point do you start thinking about your own happiness? I would have left home to go to university anyway, which is what they wanted me to do. And that dinner... Nana's last-ever birthday dinner and it was a waking nightmare, set to Vera Lynn crossed with Maroon 5.'

Claire snorted through her nose with enough force to get snot on her own top lip. She rummaged in her rucksack for a tissue, or acceptable tissue-like matter, and along with a slightly grubby napkin she found the various crumpled and piecemeal lists of Suspicious Things about the Case that she'd been working on in private. She looked at them and pursed her lips. No wonder detectives went through so many notebooks, she thought. There were so many bastard things they had to remember.

'We should make ourselves useful,' she said, 'and try to tick something off the list. Let's call those singers. The World's Most Brexit A Cappella Group.'

'LOL. The Clefs of Dover,' said Sophie. 'Good idea. I bet you don't get many results when you google *that* hot mess.'

Alex was up for it, and The Clefs had indeed cornered the internet search results in their very extreme niche. As Soph pointed out, 'It's a USP – but how many people are buying that P?'

It turned out that The Clefs had a lot of photos and a whole YouTube channel, so the three of them spent quite a while being mean about them and falling about laughing. It wasn't that they were bad singers exactly, but the task they were bending their voices to was utterly, utterly terrible. You could engage the greatest soprano in the world for a concert, but if you asked her to perform mashups of wartime hits and noughties pop songs, then that's what you'd get.

Their expressions were so uniformly earnest. Claire found the second-hand embarrassment so great that she kept trying to skip through the videos or turn them off as soon as they started playing, but Sophie wouldn't let her.

'Don't look away,' she screeched. 'Fear is the little death! Fear is the mind-killer! Permit the a cappella to pass over you and through you.'

'God, Alex, you're right,' said Claire, ignoring her. 'It *is* like looking directly at the sun. Why has nobody ever told them to stop?'

'That guy's dad definitely has,' said Alex, pointing at one, 'but he's all "The Clef's are my life, Dad!" and is convinced they'll be finalists on *Britain's Got Talent* one day.'

'They probably will,' said Claire, suddenly sobered by a vision of Glenn Miller versus Amy Winehouse getting performed in front of a glassy-eyed Prince William. 'Anyway, there's nothing on their Twitter or any blog posts about being a Clef short or anything, either.'

'I bet if one of them had been murdered by a weird family in a remote country estate, they'd be straight on to Netflix for a documentary,' said Sophie.

There was a number on their website, so Claire called it before she had time to decide it was a bad idea.

'Whoa!' Sophie exclaimed. 'We've not even discussed a game plan! What are you going to say? You can't just ask, "Excuse me, did you happen to see a murder a year ago?"'

Claire didn't respond. She put the phone on speaker and set it on the table between them.

'Claire...' said Sophie, sounding concerned. 'Claire, you do know you can't say that, don't you? Please don't say that.'

She ignored this, too. For one thing, it sounded like the sort of comment Alex *would* say.

Someone picked up the phone and said, 'Hello-oooo!' in a very sing-song voice.

'Oh, er, hello. Is that... I'm looking for...' Claire sighed. 'I'm after The Clefs of Dover.'

'Oh yes, that's me! Well, us! Ha-ha-ha!' The laugh clearly thought of itself as being like the tinkling of silver bells, but perhaps came a little closer to brassy than the owner would like. Claire imagined this was the chief Clef, the one who'd been cauliflower-cheesed. 'Would you like to book us? Our rates are—'

'Um. Sorry. No. My name's Claire, and I wanted to ask about a gig you did this time last year.'

'Oh yeah?' The Clef sounded a lot less enthusiastic. The sing-song tinkle had vanished almost entirely.

'Yeah, it's the Wellington-Forges at The Cloisters? Big weird family in a big weird house in the country? I just did a, um, a gig, I guess, for them and I'm having trouble getting paid. Someone mentioned you were there last year, and I wondered how you got on and if you had any trouble.'

Sophie looked at her in amazement. There was a crackle of static on the phone; the Clef had exhaled down the line.

'Yeah, that was *weird*, all right. I won't go into it, but that family has issues.' Alex made an it's-a-fair-cop-face, as the lead Clef went on. 'You're lucky if getting paid is the worst story you have. But as it happens, yeah, we got the runaround a bit. The guy kept saying he would get the money to us soon, offering to send a cheque. Pshh. Eventually paid us through their company instead of personally, after almost nine months.'

'Oh, wow, that's ages.'

'Yeah, I guess they wanted to try and write it off as a business expense, too, the cheeky gits. It was a pain actually, the more I think about it. Had to threaten the small claims court in the end. Total bullshit obviously, but it shook something loose. Gemma handled most of that. You should give her a ring – see if she can remember anything else.' The Clef passed on a phone number, which Alex noted down.

'That's great, thank you,' said Claire, though she was disappointed that gentle shaking of the clue-tree hadn't yielded any murder-solution fruit. Alex was paddling their hand to encourage her to keep going. 'So what was so weird about your gig, if you don't mind me asking? You all made it out okay? Ha-ha?'

'Very subtle, weirdo,' said Soph.

'Ugh! I mean, yeah, we were physically all fine, just mentally scarred. It's in the middle of nowhere, obviously – I mean, *you* know – so they told us we could stay over, which was a bit *The Hills Have Eyes*, but we charged extra for the time involved, so no biggie. Then, when we arrived, the atmos was so awkward, like they all hated each other. And the actual gig was just us singing while they ate dinner and bitched out loud. And *then* an honest-to-God food fight broke out!'

'Whoa, no waaaaaay,' said Claire, in a totally surprised tone. Alex struggled not to laugh out loud.

'Yes. I got food in my bra! Oh, that reminds me: the youngest son? Total creep. Stared at my boobs the entire time. He got punched by one of the others and I wasn't sorry about it.'

'Whoa, someone got *punched*? Who punched him?'

'I don't know – his dad, I guess? Or one of his brothers? One of the family anyway. I didn't see him get hit,' she conceded. 'But that must have been what it was. They all stormed off in different directions after dinner. A bit later we'd cleaned up and had finished loading our car, and a bunch of the men came past, propping each other up. And the dad was like, "The boys have been at a bit of horseplay", and one of the others was like, "Oh, I can't believe you hit me, Tarquin or Mumford, or whoever."' There was a pause. 'So anyway, what is it you do?'

'Oh. I'm a medium. I did a seance.'

'Huh. Nice. Very post-postmodern? I guess? How did it go?'

'Bad,' said Claire, after thinking about it.

'What happened?'

'Their nana died.'

Silence.

'Are you still there?' asked Claire, after a while.

'Yeah.'

'Okay, well. Thanks for the advice. Bye.'

She hung up and looked at Sophie, who tipped her head on one side, curls tumbling everywhere, and laughed. 'Ohmigod, don't look at me like that. You did really well. Proper private detective improvising.'

'Fucking too right,' replied Claire, satisfied by this – enough to convey Sophie's compliment to Alex.

'Yeah, the payment line was great,' Alex agreed.

'It, er, was actually based in truth. I have not been paid as yet, although I know it's only been a couple of days. Felt like a bit of a weird time to ask, to be honest.'

'Yeah, fair enough,' said Alex.

Claire called secondary Clef, Gemma, who corroborated the night's events, as well as the fact that all of The Clefs made it out alive.

'Not much going on with The Clefs, it sounds like,' said Alex. 'Good to cross them off the list.'

'I don't know about that,' said Sophie thoughtfully. 'That thing about the brothers fighting. Sounds... weird.'

'Maybe that's how Tristan ruined his suit?' suggested Claire. She suddenly felt very tired and wanted a lie-down. The throw on the sofa was quite fluffy and the cushions were nice and soft. 'I still think maybe Kevin killed Michael when he drove him out of town. I mean, that's *well* sus, isn't it?' she said, making an effort not to yawn.

Sophie pointed out that if Michael had been killed away from the house, he wouldn't be haunting it; he'd probably be wandering around a field and not bothering anyone, except the occasional psychically sensitive pigeon. Claire's argument was that if he'd been *buried* at the house, then that's where he'd be hanging about – hence the terrifying library skeleton. But she had to admit there would be no need for Kevin to drag the body all the way back there.

'I've been thinking about it anyway,' said Sophie, 'and, based on that picture you showed us, there's no way our victim can be Michael.'

'What makes you so sure?'

'If you didn't notice, then I'm not going to tell you,' said Sophie. She pouted and stuck her tongue out.

'Oh my God, you're the worst.'

Alex crawled over to lie on the floor, propping themself awkwardly against the sofa, and asked what some of the rules for ghosts and hauntings were, but Claire and Soph didn't really have any hard-or-fast answers for them. Where you died, where your body ended up or where you lived most of your life were your three best bets for where you might spend your ghostly existence, but there were exceptions. Notably Sophie. Claire didn't count on any of those three points, and yet here Sophie was.

Claire suddenly remembered her adventure in the priest-hole and told Alex about it. She fished the button out of the bottom of her backpack, but Alex shrugged. They didn't recognize it specifically; it could belong to Tuppence or Mattie or Clem, or to a guest. There was no telling how long it had been there, after all.

Solving crime was more frustrating than Claire had anticipated, although the team on *Murder Profile* did always have at least one stumbling block per episode. Maybe if she waited long enough, one day she'd figure it out. But she'd have to theorize a lot first. Preferably out loud. That always worked on *MP*.

She leaned back onto a pile of turmeric-yellow cushions and sighed. 'The killer clearly had an adolescent mindset,' she said experimentally.

Sophie stared at her and called her a weirdo. Claire did

not relate this to Alex, because they said, 'Bit weird, mate' at almost the same time.

Claire idly looked up The White Clefs of Dover on Twitter.

> OMG #clefheads. Buckle up, because I have a story for you! It starts with us being booked for a gig in the middle of nowhere, and ends with a medium killing an old lady at a seance! Strap in (1/?)

The next thing Claire knew, she was being nudged awake. She had fallen asleep somewhere around tweet number six of The Clefs' Twitter thread ('btw, Marie Claire doesn't have any tips for getting cauliflower cheese out of underwiring!'). During her nap she'd scrunched herself down so that her head was thrown back and she had probably been, at best, breathing *very* heavily in her sleep.

'You were snoring,' said Sophie's voice.

Basher was kicking Claire's feet. Her mouth tasted like she'd been sucking an old washing-up sponge, or possibly a sock. Outside, the seagulls still screamed.

'Hello,' said Basher. Claire looked at him and felt very sleepy and confused. He had changed into a cleaner, slightly less worn hoodie of light blue, and he had wet hair, so Claire surmised that he had showered. In her half-awake state, she was quietly pleased at this observation. She was definitely getting better at detectoring.

'Herk—' she croaked.

Basher, who was holding two mugs of tea, offered one to her. She tried again.

'Hello. What's happening?'

'Lunch.'

'Oh. What's for lunch?'

'A police interview.'

10

This Is the Police

Claire had been to Brighton before, but when she was quite small. She remembered a beach that was uncomfortable to sit on, and an aquarium with a depressed octopus that wouldn't come out of its pipe. These things did, Basher assured them, still exist. Although they'd probably gone through several new octopuses since then – but Basher said the current one did seem pretty depressed whenever he saw it, which was quite often. He had an annual pass to the aquarium, because he liked going there on weekdays sometimes to sit in the underwater tunnel that went through the big tank (which apparently all aquariums are legally mandated to have) and eat some sandwiches and read a book.

But Claire did not remember anything else about Brighton and, not having been there since Soph had attached herself like a spiritual mollusc or carbuncle, they both looked around with interest as they left the flat.

It was sunny, but blustery. Clouds were chasing each other across the sky so quickly that the street was flickering dark-bright-dark very quickly, like a child clicking the sun's light switch on and off to be annoying. You could see the sea from the front door of Basher and Alex's building, if you looked down the hill to the right, but it was a narrow strip of iron-grey with a lot of houses and shops in between them, and it was dotted with white bits where the wind was catching the spray. At this distance the sea wasn't the stirring, poetic sight Claire had expected. It reminded her of the bonnet of a car spackled with birdshit, in fact. She decided not to say this, and instead plumped for the traditional, if vague, 'Oh look, the sea!' because she thought that was what you were supposed to say when you saw the sea.

'Yes,' said Basher, without looking. 'The sea. I am afraid we're going this way, though.'

The four of them went left, up the hill to the other end of the street, and then set off roughly parallel to the sea, so they kept getting glimpses of it. Sophie pointed out some kind of attraction that must have been on the beach front – a giant metal pole with a big glass-and-metal doughnut-shaped thing going slowly down it. Claire thought it looked like a ring toss in slow motion, but Soph said it was 'well Freudian'.

They walked into town, past nice front gardens with gnomes and rambling roses, and side streets that had houses painted in different colours, and residential streets with those weird trees that look like angry fists because, for some reason, the council wouldn't let them grow branches. Claire noticed that a lot of the electric feeder-pillar cabinets in the street were covered in graffiti of cartoon characters saying something encouraging.

Alex peeled off, explaining that they wanted to explore the mounted dildo art idea and had got a hot lead from a Facebook group on a number of broken Big Mouth Billy Bass.

From a casual self-conducted survey of the pedestrians they walked past, Claire observed that the Brighton demographic was split pretty equally between nice old people who had been living there for decades, aggressively teenage teenagers, families with very young children, queer people with cool hair and big shoes, and people working at, or visiting, tattoo parlours.

Basher led them into a cluster of almost totally pedes-trianized shopping streets where all these people mingled together, bumping into each other and peering in the windows of independent stationery shops selling paper as thick as leather, or jewellery shops with costume brooches that looked like you could eat them, or innumerable cafés selling small-batch roasted coffee. Claire wondered how one town could sustain them all. Maybe Brightonians worked on a rota system: you do Tea for Two on Saturday, and I'll do Proper Coffee next week.

The buildings still weren't as tall as Claire was used to. Seeing that much sky at once was a bit weird and made her feel small, although not as much as the unfeeling country skies at the Wellington-Forges' estate. She knew other people felt lonely in London, but she liked it. Rather than making her feel claustrophobic or self-conscious, all the people crushed into London made her feel the opposite: relaxed and confident. There were so many other people to look at that it was unlikely anyone would pay attention to her, even if they bothered to stop worrying whether or not someone was looking at *them* (which most people didn't). She liked the Tube especially. It felt very safe, and warm. The Tube was so hot in the summer that Claire, constantly followed by her own talkative and perambulatory air-conditioning unit, reliably did feel a comfortable temperature on the Central Line at rush hour. Wandering around the weird bits of the Underground felt like what she imagined being in the womb was like.

The streets were narrower now in this bit of Brighton. There was a market on one, and Sophie diverted them by running off to have a look. She leaned over a table with a red crushed-velvet cloth, on which was dumped a mountain of unsorted silver: jewellery, charms, trinkets, scraps. Her nose was about half an inch from the heap. She was like a magpie. She liked pretty, shiny things.

Claire and Basher started poking through a bookstall nearby. He glanced at his watch, but didn't seem rushed. It struck Claire that having an actual watch and not checking the time on his phone, like everyone else these days, was the sort of deliberate choice Basher would make. She also noticed that he had nice hands. He was looking at some slightly mouldering old copies of Shakespeare's tragedies.

'You bloody *love* Shakespeare, don't you?'

'I do. There's something about his work that people can understand, especially when it's being performed. He has this amazing emotional clarity. Like when you see a video of a toddler listening to the *Moonlight Sonata* and they just *know*. And yet he invented so much at the same time. The inside of Shakespeare's head must have been amazing. But probably a nightmare to experience.'

'I think that probably applies to everyone in the world, in some ways,' said Claire. 'But I do agree with you about Shakespeare. I once saw a production of *Much Ado About Nothing* that was for, like, schools, and they changed the line 'I had rather be a canker in a hedge than a rose in his grace' to 'I had rather be a boil on a maiden's cheek than a rose in his grace' and I've never forgotten it, because of how pointless and stupid that change is.'

Basher laughed. 'Wow!'

'I know. Completely dicks the balance of the figurative language, for no reason whatsoever.'

'You did Literature too, hmm?'

'Actually I didn't. I did History. I suppose the difference now is small. Few practical applications, made fun of by STEM grads, no proper job. But I dated a guy who studied English Lit and I wanted him to like me, so for a few weeks I studied Shakespeare, too...'

Claire paused, realizing she had probably revealed too much about how strange and intense she could be, or at least had been when she was twenty. She pretended to be very interested in the other books, and thumbed through a modern romance novel. It had one of the two covers that romance novels were currently allowed to have: a cartoony rendering of modern woman in sunglasses, with the title in curly Comic Sans adjacent font; the other kind was a woman with her back to the camera in a sunhat, looking out to sea, with the title in a font meant to resemble handwriting. The implication, in either case, was usually that the woman in question was in desperate need of a man, or had one who it would turn out she did not need at all.

She bought the book. It was fifty pence and was called *The Misadventures of Lilly Addison* and, in Claire's experience, books like this were usually very good.

'Although you did,' she added, as they moved on to a table full of old *The Beano* and *The Dandy* annuals, 'have a quote-unquote proper job, I mean.'

'A lot of people would argue that I did not,' Basher replied, raising an eyebrow. His hands were back in his front pocket. 'I suppose, traditionally, the younger sons should join the clergy, shouldn't they?'

'Um. Or the military, I think. Or become lawyers.'

'Ah, well. The others have that covered. I think I only really joined the force because Mum and Dad were getting at me about, as you said, my lack of other specific prospects, and the police were desperate for bodies at the time, so you could sort of fast-track a career out of it. I didn't have a thirst for justice or anything; it just seemed easier than having to listen to Mum. I wanted to... I wanted to belong somewhere.'

'Didn't fancy getting well into *Call of Duty*?'

'I'm not really the type.'

Claire did not say that Basher didn't really seem the type to be a cop, either. 'Were you good at it?'

'Again, depends on who you ask. I am good at figuring things out, I suppose. But that is not necessarily one of your key performance indicators, as a police officer. Anyway, it turned out that Mum was even more incensed at me being unemployed than she was at me having the kind of job that anyone can do. She was just starting to imagine that I might be Police Commissioner one day, which she would find acceptable, when I packed it all in. An unforgivable betrayal, twice over.'

The next table was an assortment of bric-a-brac. There was a statuette of a cute shepherd boy in a green smock, carrying a lamb, and Claire suddenly remembered something.

'The pink shepherdess!' she cried, almost shouting. 'Nana said to tell you she kept her word about it. What does that mean?'

Basher kept looking at the table. He was otherwise incredibly still, until he reached out and, very carefully, picked up the shepherd boy. The boy had a yellow mop of curls and was frozen in the act of laughing. Basher stared into his face.

'Nana had a case of Royal Doulton figurines,' he said eventually. 'You know, the ceramic ones of women in ballgowns and children sitting on logs? I really liked them, and she let me take them out and look at them when I was little. And I dropped the pink shepherdess. Smashed it into many irreparable pieces. Nana told Mum that she broke it when she was cleaning, and we promised we'd never tell anyone. Although now, I suppose, we both have,' he said, smiling to himself, and to the shepherd boy. Basher paused again then, the smile slipping from his face. He chewed his lip and hesitated. 'Is Nana still... around?'

Claire hesitated too, wondering what it was he actually wanted to hear. 'No. She was too content with herself. Her unfinished business was asking me to figure out what happened a year ago, so I'm afraid we can't talk to her again. Er...'

Basher put the shepherd boy down slowly, but kept his hand on it. He still didn't look at her.

Claire unexpectedly felt a lump form in her throat and she coughed awkwardly. 'Um. Unless we don't figure it out, cos then maybe Nana will come back to haunt me,' she added. She felt the moment pass, the weight lift a little. 'I dunno – it's never happened before.'

Basher turned his clear grey eyes on her suddenly. 'Maybe you're not so bad, Claire,' he said.

She blushed and looked away.

He bought the green shepherd boy and carried the bag awkwardly for the rest of the day.

They moved along to another stall, this one selling comics and old annuals in individual plastic bags. Claire was surprised that such bags were allowed in a place like Brighton, where every coffee cup was reusable or biodegradable, or both. Individual plastic bags were the sort of thing that killed dolphins and ducks, but dolphins and ducks were both sexually deviant creatures, in Claire's opinion, so she didn't feel particularly aggrieved about the comics.

Sophie had wandered over now and was complaining that she was bored again. Claire blew her nose, which was both running and blocked at the same time, and looked sideways at Basher. He seemed relaxed. Like he was enjoying himself. She didn't want to ruin that, but she also thought: *What would the* Murder Profile *team do?* So she asked him about the breakfast where he had announced that he was leaving the police.

Basher rolled his neck, sighed and took a great interest in the annuals. 'Did you know,' he said, 'that the *Bash Street Kids* comic strip was originally created as *When the Bell Rings*?'

'Don't let him distract you with all his facts,' said Soph.

Claire hesitated. 'I'm not asking for The Case. I'm asking as – I dunno. A mate.'

Basher took a deep breath. 'It was terrible. It was… it was a big deal, for everyone. My job was the only thing I felt Mum and Dad could be proud of me for, if I put enough effort in. But I was miserable doing it. I got worn out. There's something rotten in the state of… here. I thought it would be noble, which sounds stupid now, but… the police catch baddies. You could make any parent proud, being a hero. Except it is mostly not doing that, even after detective training.'

Claire made a note to look up how it all worked, because she had assumed that being a detective was another rank, possibly somewhere above sergeant, but definitely below captain, because your captain was always on your ass about something. As in: 'Hello, I'm Detective Hendricks, we have to catch this serial killer soon, because the captain is on my ass about all the murders!' It was possible that *Murder Profile* was not as accurate as she had suspected. Also, it was set in America.

Basher was now flipping through copies of *The Dandy*. 'When you try to be in the in-group, you start to notice who is kept out. At least I did. But I was about the only one. And it felt as if no matter how hard I tried, I couldn't change anything. Including how Mum and Dad felt about me. I had quit before I told them, you see, but it felt like something I had to tell them in person. Like a break-up. I was dreading it. So I asked Sami to come, to *make* me.'

'I read once that if you tell someone you're going to do something, it makes you more likely to do it,' said Claire wisely. She had never told anyone she wanted to stop smoking.

'Yes, I suppose so. And I couldn't keep pretending that I was still a copper. That is a BBC2 daytime series waiting to happen. I know I'm making it sound like a massive issue, but... I was already the disappointment anyway. Mum has this weird way of... Well, I think everyone has different hang-ups about their parents, don't they?'

It wasn't rhetorical. He wanted reassurance.

'Oh, yeah. Definitely. Me and my mum don't even talk very much.'

'Neither do me and mine,' said Sophie, completely deadpan. This was true on two levels, because Sophie never asked to visit her mum. She hated the idea. It was convenient, because Sophie's mum definitely didn't want to see Claire – especially after the Essex incident put their names in the paper again.

'Sami had a go at me before breakfast about it, so that was another argument to add to the heap. She could not see why I wasn't just getting it over with. I had dragged her all the way there...' Basher went on. 'I remember sitting at the breakfast table. I was looking at the little bits of chives in my scrambled egg and instead of saying, "Could you pass the salt, please", I said, "I handed my notice in two months ago." And Mum burst into tears. She said, "How could you do this to me?", which really irritated me. Everything is about *her*, even when it really isn't. I started shouting and said she was a horrible witch who was hell-bent on controlling all of us. She said I had broken her heart, that I was ungrateful, that I'd wasted my life and everything they'd given me.'

Basher sighed heavily. 'I think that might be why I am keeping a step ahead of this – whatever this investigation is. Because while there isn't any evidence someone was killed, secretly I think... I think Mum *would* kill for one of us. Mum loves us. Very much. So much. But in a way that, I think, hurts us.' He smiled suddenly, fast and heart-breaking. 'I mean, just look at Tris.'

Soph laughed. Boys will be boys, and some boys clearly couldn't even do their own laundry.

Claire found that she had the first few lines of the chorus to 'Love Hurts' stuck in her head. She'd always assumed, when people said 'Love hurts', that they meant loving someone or something and not being able to have it, or losing it. She hadn't thought they meant that *being* loved could hurt you. Claire had a sudden urge to be open with Basher and tell him the truth about who Sophie was, and what had happened in Essex. Maybe he'd understand. He was an empathetic person, wasn't he?

She was about to open her mouth, when he did. 'We should head over, or we'll be late,' he said.

The moment was gone. Claire shoved her hand in her pocket and pulled out Sophie's pink butterfly hair-clip, which she hadn't yet tucked back away for its special seance purposes. She was finding that she liked fiddling with it – like clicking the top of a pen.

'Hey!' said Sophie. 'Careful with that. It's mine. It's... there's only one of that.'

'I know. I'm careful.'

'If you lose it—'

'I'm not going to lose it.'

They walked to a vegetarian restaurant on the next road over. It had a living wall of plants by the door and a cabinet of cakes that were many-layered and each about a foot tall.

When she arrived about ten minutes late, Sami turned out to be both very much not murdered and a smiley British Indian woman, with a gap between her front teeth that only made her smile nicer. Her black hair was tied back into a loose bun, but it looked like it was cut so that she could easily pin it back into a style of shining professionalism. Her eyes were kind, but also lively and quick, taking in everything. She noted, for example, the brief wince that Claire made as she looked at the prices on the menu.

'I assume you'll be treating us to lunch, *Sebastian*, since you're clearly about to ask me a favour,' she said, grinning. 'He is, isn't he?'

'I don't know,' said Claire, who realized too late that she hadn't asked anywhere near the number of questions about Sami that an inquisitive detective should.

When Basher and Alex had described Sami as Basher's partner, Claire had assumed it was as in 'girlfriend', which she was now realizing was incorrect. Sophie pointed out that Sami was wearing a ring, and her clothes were covered in small sticky thumbprints and bits of food, the everyday accessories of parents of a toddler. Sami was actually Detective Sergeant Sami Wilson, Basher's old *police* partner, which now seemed very obvious. After the successful Case of the Man Who Had a Shower Recently, Claire demoted herself down to a mere amateur detective for making an assumption.

'Oh, wait, um... Can I see your ID, you know?' Claire asked.

Sami smiled indulgently and produced her warrant card – she even had it in one of those flippy-open holders, like on the TV.

'Thanks. Always wanted to see one,' Claire said. In fact it confirmed Sami's identity. So now she could be

211

almost 100 per cent sure that Basher was trustworthy, or at least had not killed his former partner. Which was a great relief.

'It is for a bit of a favour that I asked you here, I'm afraid,' said Basher. 'And a... well, a slightly strange one.'

'You going to ask me how I am, first?'

'How are you?'

'All right. You?'

'Nana died.'

The smile instantly dropped from Sami's face. 'Oh god, Bash. I'm sorry. Of course I'll help. Whatever you need.'

Basher hesitated. 'Well, it's not... If I am being totally honest, it is not directly about that. That's just the headline of what has been happening to me lately.'

'I see,' said Sami, the smile cautiously creeping back, like a cat coming out from under a sofa. 'So that was to make me feel like an arsehole for demanding lunch. I activated your trap-card. You can definitely pay now.'

'Yes, yes, all right. It is tangentially related, though. Nana only died a couple of days ago, but she told Claire something...' Basher paused. He seemed to be thinking of the best way to proceed. How to frame what The Case actually was.

'Don't say anything,' Sophie advised. Claire nodded.

'You remember her birthday last year? Well, Nana told Claire that she thought someone was killed that weekend. I er... I think she might have seen a body.'

Sami was shocked. She half laughed. 'What... really?'

'Yes. Seriously.'

Basher outlined what had happened, although he made it seem like the conversation had taken place before Nana had died.

'Are you asking me to try and open a case?' asked Sami. 'Because—'

'No! No, of course not. There's nothing to report to anyone. There are no signs of a body *now*. Or anything, really. But Nana trusted Claire, and I trust Nana.'

'And I trust you, I suppose,' said Sami. She rolled her eyes and sighed. 'So what do you actually want?'

'I want to check out the other guests who were there that weekend. They have been quite hard to track down.'

'Oh, is that *all*,' said Sami, 'just a casual invasion of privacy, based on hearsay?'

'I do not mean address and blood type, plus inside leg; merely, you know, check there aren't any open Missing Persons cases or reports from concerned relatives. And then nobody has to think about it ever again.' Basher spread his hands appealingly. 'I want to rest easy, knowing that my family did not kill anyone.'

'I don't think he'll ever be able to do that,' said Sophie tartly.

Sami raised her eyebrows and said Basher would definitely owe her more than a lunch after this, but her manner became a bit more businesslike. 'Was Nana making sense? She wasn't confused?'

There was a long pause while Claire worked out that Sami was talking to her. 'Oh, uh, yeah. She was fine. Sharp as the proverbial tack.'

'Did she say where she saw the body?'

'Um... in the library. But I think it was more like, you know, remains. She couldn't tell who it was.'

'Why did she tell you this?'

'I dunno, really. I think she liked us – er, me. I think she liked *me*.'

Sami looked quite hard at Claire for a few seconds. 'All right,' she said eventually. She opened a notepad, although not, Claire saw, an official police one. 'Give me their names, Basher. I'm not promising *anything*, mind you,' she added, pointing her pen at him sternly. She slid both the notepad and the pen over to him.

'I wouldn't ask you to,' said Basher. 'Thanks, Sami.'

'Yeah, yeah,' she replied. Basher wrote down three names and pushed the pad back. Sami started adding her own notes . 'Oh, I hope you don't think I'm being rude, Claire, but why were you there?'

'Oh, I was the entertainment. Er, this year's Clefs of Dover.'

Sami laughed at this.

'Don't tell her what you do,' said Sophie quickly. 'Make something up. Anything.'

'What do you do?' Sami asked, on cue.

Claire was again unable to think on her feet. 'I'm actually a medium,' she confessed. 'I was going to do a seance. You know, sort of spooky, for Halloween.'

Sami nodded. She did not ask anything else, or look up from writing, or make any comment at all. This was strange. People usually at least went, 'Cool!' in a polite and insincere way, such as they might respond to someone saying, 'I'm a taxidermist' or 'I make small sculptures out of boiled eggs'.

Then the notebook was put away, and Sami went back to not seeming at all like a police officer. Claire ordered the soup of the day, which turned out to be some kind of spicy sweet potato thing. She asked Sami if she remembered anything from that weekend.

'Well, I don't think I'll ever forget that dinner,' she said. 'It was intense.' She gave a brief summary of her memories of the dinner, which were basically in line with Alex's, but more concentrated at her end of the table.

'Yes, my family are quite odd,' said Basher. His air was a bit apologetic.

'Actually,' said Sami, 'apart from the food-hurling, I'd say they were fairly typical of families of their type. If that's any consolation.'

The expression on Basher's face indicated that it was not.

'Did anything else weird happen that weekend?' Claire asked. 'Did you hear anything after dinner?'

Sami shook her head. 'I sleep with headphones in. And the dinner does overshadow most of my other memories, to be honest. I remember seeing Figgy and her boyfriend – whatshisname, the awful one – arguing before that. You were sitting in the garden doing your sad act, remember, Bash? It was just before four o'clock.'

'Told you!' Basher said to Claire, with a note of triumph. 'Timeline wobbles. The weekend does not all match up,' he added to Sami, by way of explanation.

'Still doesn't match up,' Claire mumbled into her spoon.

'There was one thing, actually,' Sami said suddenly.

'Was it to do with Michael? The accountant guy?'

'Ohmigod, I told you, it's so not him,' said Sophie.

'No, not him – he spent the whole time avoiding me, if anything,' Sami went on. 'No, it was the housekeeper. Mattie. She pulled me aside on the Saturday and asked if we could have a private chat. But then your mum came down the hall and she clammed up. Never saw her alone again. Or at all.'

'You never mentioned that,' said Basher.

'I assumed it was about you, or something. Mattie was a bit nervous, but not sweating bullets or anything. You should ask Alex's mum about her, actually. Whenever anyone made a round of tea, Tuppence would always take a cup to Mattie in the office. Probably chatted a bit.'

After they'd finished lunch, Sami had to get home to help her husband with their two- and four-year-olds, describing the former as a 'fucking tyrant', but she thanked them for giving her a reason to get out and about by herself. Sophie asked Basher, via Claire, if they could go and see the depressed octopus.

Brighton aquarium purported to be the oldest aquarium in the world that was still operating. It was underground, and gave off quite Victorian Gothic vibes inside. It was as if Dracula had suffered in the economic crash and had to sell his holiday dungeon, and the Sea Life people had snapped it up.

It was dark and quiet. At the end of one long, low room there was a circular tank of jellyfish. They were zooming around it in a spiral in an unseen current. It looked like someone had put a bunch of carrier bags into a washing machine.

'I feel sick,' said Soph.

'You don't have a stomach,' said Claire automatically.

'They do actually!' said a dead teenager in an aquarium polo shirt, who had clearly been waiting hours for this very moment and appeared so suddenly he made Claire go 'Argh'. He went on, 'It's a very simplified one, very different from the stomach you have.'

'She was talking about me, not about the jellyfish,' said Sophie. The boy shrugged and walked off and into one of the tanks, where he stood, distorted by the thick glass and water, looking at the huge fish swimming around and through him with interest. 'God, that looks quite creepy,' said Sophie. 'I might try it.'

Claire scuttled over to the tank on the opposite wall, which turned out to be the depressed octopus's. Mission accomplished! It was squished inside a pipe, styled to look like a water valve, which was the only thing in the tank. Claire imagined there was a nicer half of the tank kept secret from the public that had enrichment toys in it, where the octopus could play football, or whatever octopuses did on their downtime.

The only things visible were some anaemic tentacles poking out, and the suggestion of a baleful yellow eye in the darkness.

'Fucking hell,' said Soph.

Two other employees were talking quietly nearby. 'She's not doing well today, no,' said one. Claire realized he meant the octopus. 'Probably only a few months left, they say.'

'Ohmigod. Most depressing octopus ever. Ten out of ten.'

Basher had ambled over to stand next to them. All three – *four* – stayed there in silence for a bit.

'You know,' said Sophie conversationally, 'I couldn't read Basher's writing, but Sami added a name to the list. She has very neat handwriting. She wrote your name down. She's going to look you up. She's going to find out.'

Claire stood rooted to the spot, maintaining eye contact with the sickly octopus.

'Big,' she said eventually, 'mood.'

11

The Sesh

The flat didn't have a third bedroom, or one of those inflatable mattresses that are only really used at Christmas, and which slowly deflate over the course of the night so that in the morning the occupant is sleeping on the floor anyway. Instead, Alex added some pillows and a blanket to the sofa. Claire and Sophie slept the sleep of the dead – i.e. they did not, instead flipping between analysing clues and watching reels of the worst-case scenarios of Sami looking up Claire's name playing out behind her eyes.

Eventually the sun came up again, which made it Monday. This would have been a complication, except that nobody currently in the flat had what would traditionally be thought of as a real job. Accordingly, when Claire woke up from a fitful doze, it was after eleven. She found Alex carefully clearing space on the cluttered coffee table so they could put down a mug of tea. Claire sat up to drink it, with something of the air of a stray cat sniffing at a kind stranger's hand. Basher walked in from the kitchen, and Claire scrabbled to get under the blankets again, because she didn't have any jeans on. Soph laughed, but Basher hadn't even glanced at her. His nose was in an open recipe book, and he was tapping a biro on his chin.

'We could make some stuffed apples properly,' he said. 'They make a nice cold-weather dessert with cream. But that would need a lighter main. Maybe salmon... Well, whatever the case, we shall need to go into town to get some supplies.'

'What about the murder investigation?' asked Sophie. Claire echoed this. Surely there were pressing things to be done.

'Uncle Bash says it'll take a few days to hear back from Sami anyway. So we might as well have a nice time,' said Alex. They sat on the floor and patted the space in front of them. 'Here, c'mere, S. I want to see if I can feel it if we do pat-a-cake.'

Basher sat by the coffee table and produced a notepad, on which he started to write a careful list of things he needed to buy, with amounts in brackets.

Claire started to say 'Um...' but Basher waved a hand towards the kitchen without looking up. 'There is bread for toast, and cereal in the cupboard above the kettle,' he said. 'And I have hung a clean towel on the back of the bathroom door.'

Claire had a shower and put the same jumper on for the fourth day in a row. She stopped at the doorway to the living room and looked in. The room was full of weak autumn light. Basher now seemed to be making a duplicate of his shopping list in an app on his phone. Alex had their hands up for Sophie to hit at them, and they were both giggling. Claire stood there watching for a long time, until Basher looked up and said, 'Oh, are we all ready to go then?'

They walked into town in a different direction from before, and ended up at a covered market. They bought some thin fillets of salmon at the fishmonger's, where Claire eyed the blank fishy faces staring up at her from a bed of ice with extreme suspicion, in case one of them moved. She had not yet seen an animal ghost, but shops like that seemed the most likely place.

At the greengrocer's Alex talked to Sophie out loud, as if they could hear her, and without any worry about what other people might think. 'We need at least four of these, S, but probably six, to be safe. What about this one? Or this?' They held huge green apples into the air for invisible approval. Basher called Claire over to ask if she preferred green beans or sugar-snap peas, sultanas or raisins.

Basher turned out to be a very enthusiastic cook. It was oddly exhilarating watching him – an intentionally drab person – light up from the inside to the out as he mixed together double cream and raisins and rum, rubbed rich butter into flour, and used twice as much garlic and chilli as the recipe suggested to stir-fry green beans to go with the salmon. He only put up a cursory objection to Alex insisting that he plated up a portion of everything for Sophie as well. They pretended to be a fancy maître d', tea towel over their forearm, as they put down the huge stuffed apple, swimming in cream, in front of where Sophie was sitting. She beamed. It was delicious.

That night Claire dreamed that she woke up the next day in a bed. In her dream, Basher came in and said they didn't have anything to do today, either. She went and sat on the sofa and he brought her a bowl of chicken soup.

She was almost surprised when she woke up on the sofa and saw that, while there wasn't any soup, Alex had again left a cup of tea on the coffee table for her. She was even more surprised when, just after she had finished a plate of what Basher told her was butternut-squash risotto for lunch, the ancient buzzer screamed like a modem shagging a blender, and a crackling robot version of Tristan's voice announced that he was outside. This was an unexpected development, especially on a weekday. Alex seemed suspicious.

'I'm suspicious,' they said, buzzing Tristan in. 'Dad wouldn't simply let him have an afternoon off work. I bet he's here as an undercover agent.'

'Bet they're right,' said Soph. 'We're lucky Tristan isn't the sharpest tool in the proverbial. He'll be even less subtle than you would.'

Tristan entered in a suit and slightly loosened tie, accessorized with a home-made wool scarf that he was obviously under maternal orders to wear when it was cold. After saying hello, he flopped down on the sofa and, as if he had overheard Sophie and specifically wanted to prove her right, said, 'So, Claire. Bloody hell! Ghosts and stuff. How long have you been doing that? Ever met any murder victims or anything cool?' He did not seem surprised to see her, or to consider that maybe he should have pretended to be surprised to see her. Claire wondered how Tristan had known she was there.

She smiled and was vague, although she always was when people asked her for exactitudes on her job. 'Only been doing the medium thing full-time for a few years really, but I've been able to see and talk to ghosts since I was a teenager.'

'Oh yah, cool, like the X-Men,' he said, with much enthusiasm.

'Yes,' replied Claire, calibrating her tone to better suit, for example, a Labrador who was not following proceedings exactly, but could stay on task with encouragement, 'like the X-Men.'

Basher walked in and displayed no visible surprise at Tristan's appearance, although Claire noticed a fractional pause in his stride towards the kitchen.

'Good afternoon, Tris,' he said mildly. 'To what do we owe the pleasure? Can I get you a cup of tea? Coffee?'

'Mate, I can answer *both* of those questions by taking you down the pub. It's been so long since we had a proper sesh, you know?'

'On a Tuesday? Just like that? Why?'

Tris appeared to fumble when called upon to improvise. Claire had some sympathy. 'Why not?' he said eventually.

'Because I am nearly thirty and if I get tanked on a Tuesday I had better not have any other plans until Friday?'

'Speak for yourself,' said Alex. 'I'll come out with you, Uncle T. Life is short.'

'Yeah, exactly!' said Tris, grasping with visible relief at this lifesaver. 'I've been thinking about, er, life. Because of Nana. *Carpe diem* and all that.'

'Interesting,' said Basher, calling through from the kitchen. 'And it's only you, is it?'

'Like, who else would it be? Figgy is staying with the 'rents, by the way. Bit of a state still.'

Claire absorbed this information and silently looked over at Sophie, who shrugged. 'I mean, did any of us really think Figgy had the mental fortitude to do and/or cover up a murder?'

And when she thought about it, no, Claire really couldn't believe that Figgy was involved. She was too surface-level. And, she realized, watching Tristan's forehead wrinkle in time with every thought that formed behind it, so was Tristan, but this pub sesh might provide an opportunity to get more information. She could play good cop, and lull Tristan into a false sense of security by slamming a Jägerbomb with him.

Basher re-entered from the kitchen carefully eating a Custard Cream, one corner at a time, and stared at his brother. Then he tossed one at Tristan, who caught it and grinned. It seemed to be some kind of obscure, silent peace ritual, because then Basher said, 'Yes, all right then. Coming, Claire?'

'Er, yeah, okay. Bit early to get started, though, isn't it?'

'It's the sesh, mate! The *sesh*,' said Tristan, awkwardly punching her on the shoulder. 'Afternoon pre-game, yah?'

They all put on jackets and jumpers, which they would regret putting on once they got hot on the walk, and headed out.

'Most perverted way to eat a Custard Cream I have ever seen,' said Sophie, watching the back of Basher's head. He was talking to Tristan. 'Bet he's into some weird sex stuff. One hundred per cent freak.'

'Like you'd know!' muttered Claire, blushing, as Basher dropped back to talk to her, letting Alex and Tristan lead the way.

'I, er, think I might know why Tristan is here,' he said. He looked a bit sheepish. 'He told me Monty says hello, and to remember to tidy my room. Which is Monty having a dig. You remember the big flipchart that Alex put up in my room?'

'The one with a heading saying "Potential Victims" on it? And a list of their names?'

'That's the one. The thing is that I *didn't* remember it...'

Sophie groaned. 'Oh *no-o-o*, that house of chicken-fucker psychos found a giant flashing neon sign saying, "You are suspected of doing a bad murder."'

'That's not great, is it?' said Claire.

'No. And it is also not good that Tris has been sent here.'

'I dunno, I think we're lucky that your mum doesn't have a strong hand of cards to play,' said Claire, watching as Tristan almost walked into a lamp post because he was looking at one of his phones, and being pulled out of the way by Alex at the last moment.

'True,' replied Basher, half smiling, 'but that's not what I meant. If nothing happened, the list would just have confused Mum and Dad. But it seems it didn't. Tristan's appearance smacks of guilt. So I am not thrilled at this turn of events, you see.'

Claire saw. 'I'm sure it'll be all right, one way or another,' she said after a pause. 'Things usually are, aren't they?'

'"Everything's for the best, in the best of all possible worlds",' Basher said and smiled at her very nicely. Sophie cleared her throat sarcastically, and Claire's tummy swooped. She tried to ignore both.

They arrived at a pub that was covered with shiny green ceramic tiles on the outside, which gave Claire the impression that it was either upside down or inside out. The interior was full of hanging plants in copper bowls and exposed light bulbs, and very few people. There was a pause as Alex tried, unsuccessfully, to get Tris to open a tab on his company credit card. They almost managed it, but ultimately Tristan's abiding fear of Monty's wrath outweighed his desire to be liked – although he got the first round in, as a compromise. At Alex's urging, this included two bottles of wine and a tray of sticky layered shots, as well as Tristan's pint and a fizzing whiskey ginger for Basher. He drew circles on the sweating glass with his finger, while Claire surveyed the shots with rising alarm.

'Seems a lot for this early on a Tuesday...'

'Well, if you're going to do something wrong, do it right,' said Alex, cheerful and unrepentant.

'Oh, to be young again,' murmured Basher.

Sophie cupped her chin in her hand and sighed. 'I hate it when you get hammered. You have no idea how boring drunk people are, when you're sober. You all just yell and repeat yourselves and fall over.'

Tristan raised his glass and gave a 'Chin-chin!', so Claire gave a half-shrug and took a gulp of wine. What seemed like a very short time later, she noticed that she was feeling much more relaxed, and the entire glass of wine was empty. The outing suddenly didn't seem like such a bad idea.

When it became clear that Tristan wasn't going to *immediately* admit that he or members of his family had killed someone, Sophie got bored and fidgety. She started wandering around the bar and eavesdropping on the staff and the scant few other customers. Alex had obviously been thinking along the same lines as Claire, because they were palming most of the shots off on Tristan. He was getting louder, and his pale cheeks bloomed with two little ruddy-pink patches – the ghost of Hugh yet to come. As he mixed more sticky, brightly coloured drinks with cold fizzing lager, it was as if Tristan, too, began to effervesce. He talked a lot about lads from the office who all had nicknames that were their last names suffixed with -y or -ers or -o (as in: Smithy, Campers and Gibbo), and then, gradually, began to complain about the workload and about how strict Monty was.

The problem, Claire thought, as she noticed that her brain and her body were about a second out of sync – her thoughts a toddler wearing those elasticated reins, and her skull the lumpen parent holding it back – was that the rest of them weren't drinking *no* drinks at the same time as they were funnelling them into Tristan.

'Hey,' she said suddenly, 'hey, who's going to be the... you know – designated driver?'

Tristan frowned. 'We're not driving anywhere,' he said, quite reasonably.

'Yeah, but I mean, like, who's *in charge*,' said Claire, trying to look significantly at Alex, who was developing a definite list to one side.

'It's fine, C, I am totally in control. One. Hundred. Percentiles,' they said, angled at about one o'clock.

Claire looked to her left. Basher was smiling a lot and had bought a sharing packet of Doritos from behind the bar.

'I remember them. Remember you eating them, I mean. At a party at our uni,' she said.

'What uni? Oh, Figgy's? Yes, I visited,' Basher replied. He squinted at her. 'Your hair was different.'

Claire said, 'So was yours' and that made Basher laugh again. She was okay with that.

Alex went and ordered more drinks. Claire realized *she* was going to have to be the adult, which didn't seem like a recipe for success. But she was still sober enough to realize that, which meant it was probably fine, right? In fact she was pretty sure she was sober enough that she could safely have another drink. She continued thinking this for some time, until suddenly she noticed it was dark and she was in the queue for a karaoke bar near the seafront.

Basher was next to her. He kept singing the first lines of the chorus of 'Sweet Caroline' at an enthusiastic volume.

'Sweeeet Caroline!'

Claire blinked slowly. She was supposed to do something here. 'WHOA-OH-*OOOHHH!*' she offered.

Basher threw a delighted arm over her shoulder. 'Not so bad. Not so bad at all, hmm?' he said.

Claire, against all probability, giggled.

'You're wrecked,' said Sophie.

'M'not,' said Claire, before remembering she wasn't supposed to talk to Soph out loud. There were people around who weren't in the know. Claire tried to tap her nose and missed. She focused on Tristan, who was standing nearby. He was smoking with deep concentration, his eyes almost closed. He was wobbling slightly. This reminded Claire of the purple dildo and made her laugh a lot.

'We should. We should get you a purple suit, Tristan. Hey, Tristan. Hey, Tris! You should get a purple suit.'

Tristan smiled happily at her. He was all right, Tristan. Just stupid. But lots of people were stupid. Like the man said – the seven-words-on-TV man. Think of how stupid the average person is. He had a good point. You can't put people in prison for being stupid. The prisons aren't big enough.

Alex staggered back over.

'Here,' they slurred. 'Couple of my mates are' – they paused to stifle a burp – 'my mates are in a room. C'mon.'

'I thought you didn't have many mates,' said Claire.

Alex stopped and stared at her imperiously, if without focus, for a few seconds. 'I have at least two,' they said eventually and led them all inside.

'Wow. Drunk Alex is a... is a... is an *arsehole*,' said Claire. Basher heard this and laughed, and half picked Claire up in a squeeze. 'Drunk Basher is a hugger,' she added.

'Yes! Yes, yes, I'm a hugger. Big hugs,' he replied, turning to hug his brother as well.

'George Carlin!' Claire suddenly yelled triumphantly.

'Wh... what?'

'S'nothing. Never mind.'

They trooped into a dark, hot, upholstered box with a screen at one end and a bench running around three of the walls, while Sophie muttered expletives and *ohmigods* under her breath. The chill of her presence did immediately make the karaoke booth a less oppressive place. There were vague humanoid shapes already taking up most of the space in it, two of which hugged Alex and nearly fell over. Everyone else was singing 'Come On Eileen'. Someone tried to introduce themselves, but Claire only heard *WOMP-WOMP-WOMP-WOMP*. She started singing instead and was immediately enveloped into the group. She couldn't see any of the others. Except sometimes someone with blue hair or grey eyes would scream lyrics happily in her face. Sophie alternated between standing next to Alex and singing, if it was a song she liked, and sitting in the corner and sulking. All the beer was in plastic bottles and got hot too quickly. It tasted awful. After 'Don't Stop Me Now' was over, Claire went outside to be sick. It was the most fun she'd ever had in her life.

She was sick behind a car over the road. She was pleased to see it was an Audi. Ha-ha. Take that! She leaned back to look up at the sky and nearly fell over a bin, so she sat down on the kerb. It was cold. Her breath caught in her throat. But it was nice cold.

'I'm the king of the world,' she yelled at nobody in particular, still looking upwards. 'I'm never going to die!'

Claire saw that a bouncer outside the bar was looking at her with quiet amusement. He offered a light to a man who stumbled outside, and Claire realized the man was Tristan. She waved at him and he came over. He, too, sat down very heavily on the kerb. They looked at each other muzzily.

'So what—'

'Did you—'

Claire realized they were both making a last-ditch attempt to intro... interior... in terror... interrogate each other. She laughed.

'S'okay, Tris,' she said, graciously. 'You go first.'

Tristan opened his mouth, then paused, and looked confused again. 'Oh. I forgot.' He giggled to himself. 'Oh my *God,* that is *so* un*fair*! Never mind, old chap, never mind. Dad'll sort it.'

'Hey, Tristan,' Claire said, as he started to slump against her side. 'Tristan, what happened that night?'

'What night?'

'*You* know. That night last year. The party.'

'Oh yah. We're s'posed to talk about that. Well, I'm not, but you are.' His expression suddenly crumpled and he looked forlorn. 'Terrible. Horrible business. Wish I hadn't been there.' He sniffed like he was about to cry and turned into her shoulder.

'Hey. S'okay, man,' she said. 'S'not your fault.'

Tristan sat up and rubbed his nose, making a very snotty noise. 'That's right. That's right. I just do what I'm told, don't I?'

Claire felt her head going a bit dizzy. She shook herself and noticed that Sophie had wandered out, probably looking for her, and was walking over to listen. Claire pulled herself together as much as was possible and tried again.

'What happened to your... your suit?'

'Purple one?'

'No, you... do you have a purple one? No, the muddy one.'

'Mate. Can't blame me for falling over. It was all rainy and slippery.'

'Why were you outside if it was so wet?'

'Mum was livid – she said it'd never get properly clean. Can't blame a man. If someone shoves him, you know?'

'Aaah-*HA!*' Claire shouted, pointing a finger at him. 'Gotchu there. Who shoved? You said before that you fell, but you just said you got shoved. Caught you!'

'No one shoved me.'

'But you *said*.'

'Well, what's the difference anyhow?' he said defensively.

'Pretty big difference actually,' said Claire. She noted that Sophie was watching with a similar expression to the bouncer. Detached, but amused.

'You're pretty,' said Tristan out of nowhere. He lunged at her with amorous intent. Claire went, 'Eugh, fuck off' and put a hand across his entire face to push him away. He flopped happily onto the pavement.

'See,' said Claire, looking at Sophie and pointing at the prone Tristan. 'That was a—' She stopped, leaned to the other side and was sick again. '*That* was a shove.'

12

Working from Home

Basher's prediction was correct, in that when they all woke up on Wednesday morning, he and Claire were monstrously hungover. Tristan, who had slept in Basher's room, had gone to the train station before Claire had even approached consciousness, and she couldn't imagine what that journey would feel like. Alex confidently declared that they were minutes from death, was very noisily sick in the bathroom and then was absolutely fine to do their shift at the library. Then Basher also went out, because he had a lunchtime shift at a pub.

'I'm going to walk along the beach first,' he said, as he was going. 'With any luck I shall be found frozen to death on the waterline before I am called upon to do anything.'

Claire asked if he wouldn't prefer to cancel his shift, but Basher said he preferred to be doing something, so that he couldn't dwell on... anything, including the most immediate feeling that his frontal lobe was gently dissolving – and could Claire please not go into his room while he was gone, thank you; there's a spare key in the kitchen drawer with all the batteries in it. It was only after everyone else had left that the paracetamol started to kick in and Claire, staring balefully at herself in the mirror as she brushed her teeth, remembered that she had uncovered some important new Clues regarding The Case the night before.

Sophie didn't mind when they were left alone in someone else's house. She was always able to behave, within the specific limitations of her condition, exactly as she wanted. And did. She wasn't used to a flat with such huge windows and when Claire went into the front room, Sophie was sitting cross-legged on the coffee table in beams of sunshine, looking curiously at her own self becoming see-through. It made her look a bit like a faded photocopy of herself. Like the missing posters of her that had gone up on lamp posts and telephone poles around town.

Claire, on the other hand, did not like being left alone in other people's houses; no matter how much the occupant would impress upon her that she really could make herself at home, she always felt like this was not really the case.

Say if she got hungry and she decided to make a sandwich: she couldn't shake the feeling that someone would leap out from behind a corner and have a go at her, for using too much butter. If you are somewhere you can't make yourself lunch without being concerned the entire time that you might be using the Special Ham – and that later there would be an awkward conversation, where Basher asked where his ham was, and then said it was totally fine that she'd eaten the ham, but several times and with a *tone* – then you aren't anywhere that is home to you.

But what made it more obviously a lie was that in her own home Claire could sit around in her pants or without a bra on, gnawing on a hunk of cheese like an animal, because there were too many steps involved in making an actual meal (and also cheese is nice). Clearly this sort of thing is not allowed in someone else's house. For this reason, Claire did make a sandwich, because she was hungry, but almost immediately retrieved the spare key and told Sophie they were going out.

Sophie shrugged. 'Where to?'

'The aquarium,' said Claire decisively, naming one of about three places in Brighton that she could remember how to get to.

They walked down to the sea and along the front, past the remains of another pier that had burned down decades before and were now barely keeping together out at sea – a collection of ribs sticking out of the water. The beach was home to a small but not statistically insignificant collection of ghosts, mostly sad people in swimming suits from different decades, or sailory types in woolly jumpers. These lads strolled around in twos or threes, discussing whether or not it looked like a storm was coming in.

When Claire and Sophie arrived at the aquarium, however, Claire ran into a problem that hadn't presented itself when she went there with Basher, which was that it cost £30 to get in. She hovered in the entrance nervously, trying not to catch the eye of the woman behind the till, and was about to turn round and go home when she distinctly heard someone go, 'Pssst!'

'Er...' She looked around.

'Pssst!'

'Oh! It's the water-boy from the other day,' said Soph. 'Look, he's hiding round the corner. For some reason.'

Claire looked. Sophie was right; the teenage jellyfish enthusiast was peering round the wall that led to the aquarium proper, on the other side of the ticket barrier.

'Pretend to be looking in your bag for your pass,' he hissed, once he saw that he had Claire's attention. 'Then get a card out. Any card – doesn't matter.'

She did as she was told, feeling a bit stupid. She even said, 'Ah, there it is!' as she got out an old train ticket, in case the living employee was bothered.

The water-boy dropped to the ground and commando-crawled to the ticket barriers. He got into a crouch and beckoned Claire over. 'Pretend to swipe it,' he said in a stage whisper. As Claire did so, the boy stuck his hand into the guts of the machine and the light on it blinked green. She pushed through the gate.

'Thank you,' she said.

'Anything for a lady,' he replied. He puffed up his chest a bit. 'I'm not supposed to, but my manager told me we can use discretion to bring in special guests sometimes.'

'Yeah, thanks,' said Soph, looking at him out of the corner of her eye. 'What was all that spy stuff about, though? You know they can't see you?'

He deflated a little. 'I suppose some habits... well – you know.'

They walked on. After a bit the boy jogged to catch up.

'My name's Elton,' he said. Claire was incredulous, but Elton was obviously used to this. 'My mum was a big fan of his,' he explained.

'Didn't ask,' said Sophie. She sniffed.

Elton grinned. He was evidently a man who wasn't going to let a rare opportunity pass by when it turned up dead in front of him. Claire noticed that, if you looked closely, the polo shirt he was wearing wasn't the same shade of blue as the ones the living aquarium employees had on. Elton himself was tall but a bit gangly with it, wore his hair in boy-band curtains and had unfortunately brought a couple of spots on his chin into the afterlife.

Claire went to the depressed octopus's tank and looked in at the sad eye in the pipe, but kept one ear on the conversation happening next to her.

'I died in a car crash in 1992 when I was eighteen,' Elton explained. 'But I'm, like, fully over it now. I was going to be a marine biologist and now I'm continuing my studies on a – you know – ad hoc basis. What about you?'

'None of your beeswax,' said Soph. 'But I was seventeen, in case you wanted to know.'

This part-schoolyard bickering, part-banter continued as they walked around the rest of the aquarium. Eventually they came to a dark room, where a motion-sensitive camera demonstrated luminescence in sea algae by lighting up a section of floor when you walked across it. There were wave sounds playing over a speaker.

'Here, look,' said Elton. He grabbed Sophie's hand and pulled her along under the camera, and after a delay of a few seconds the lights worked, blooming under their feet. 'Cool, huh? Some things can tell we're still here. Sort of.'

A couple of tourists who'd been trying the lights out nearby decided that it must be broken and walked away.

'My name's Sophie,' said Sophie. She kept looking down at her feet. They were bathed in pale blue lights.

'Nice to meet you, Sophie,' said Elton. 'We could, you know, meet up at the café sometime next week? If you wanted?'

Sophie abruptly dropped his hand. She seemed to be speechless for a moment. This eventuality had not occurred to her.

'I don't think I'll be here then,' she managed. 'C'mon, let's get out of here, Claire. We should get back.'

They tramped back up the hill and into the flat, Sophie resolutely refusing to talk about Elton the entire time.

By the time they arrived it was after four, and Basher and Alex were both home.

Alex said they had spoken to Tristan and he claimed not to remember anything from the night before, which reminded Claire that she did recall some things – and that Sophie could fill in the bits she didn't. So she recounted what Tristan had said about being shoved.

'Yes, I've been thinking,' said Alex, after seeing off a pint of Berocca, 'about the murder.' They were lying in their habitual position: full-length on the floor, neck crooked up against the sofa, legs at weird angles. 'I have some new ideas. Like, we can send a DM to Kevin. I already called Dad's firm, so we can also go up there and look for clues about Michael – that needs to happen. And I know Mattie isn't answering her phone, but didn't you say you were at school with her kid, Uncle B?'

'Mmm,' said Bash, who was slumped on the other end of the sofa with a tea towel on his face. 'So? Ugh. Oh God, I feel dreadful. Weep for Adonais – he is dead!'

'So, look him up on Facebook! I bet you're friends on there, so you can check that nobody you went to school with is much more happy and successful than you are. That's what Facebook is for, right? At what point do we not simply admit that most police work could be done via webcam?'

Basher waved them away and said he would message the man now.

'*I* was thinking,' said Soph, warming to the theme, 'of what we were saying about the body the other day – how it must be at The Cloisters somewhere. Well, *where*? It's not in the library.'

Claire was frankly disgusted that Alex was able to move, let alone think, and resented the fact that Soph was acting as an accomplice, but she still emptied out her Case Notes and started arranging them in some sort of order.

The body couldn't be in the house, she reasoned, or at least was unlikely to be, because there had been a whole year's worth of corporate retreats and weddings kicking about there. Someone would have noticed the smell, so inside the house wasn't a safe place. Unless they'd misjudged everything and they were actually in a horror movie situation, and Hugh and Clem were running a meat farm so that the rich could eat pies made of people instead of chicken, the body was probably somewhere in the grounds. The trouble was that a large expanse of the place was a lawn, and you can only blame moles for so much.

'Well, look, Tristan definitely knows something,' said Claire. 'He said he was pushed over, right? And the Clef told us that they saw the brothers "propping each other up" after a fight. What if they saw some combination of lads carrying a body into the house? Then they stashed it in the library until you two and Sami were out of the way. Then, according to our timeline, they only had an afternoon to put the vic in its final resting place before a bunch of Hooray Henries turn up for business-approved bonding during the week, right?'

'That's pretty good,' said Alex. 'So the vic must have been Michael or Kevin, right? The Clef said they were propping up another man.'

'*Unless* they dressed Mattie in Tristan's suit in the garden as a disguise, and that's how it got all muddy,' said Claire. 'You know, rolling the body around, trying to stuff the arms in and all that.'

'You *just* said Tristan let slip that he was pushed,' said Sophie. 'So that has to be the way his suit got muddy. Someone pushed Tristan over.'

'Oh yeah. Wow, this is a tough one, isn't it? I wish we'd had a proper look round before we left,' Claire added, with the air of a seasoned investigator. 'For signs of, er... turned earth. Or things like that.'

'Ah yes, things of that nature. May I remind you that you were very eager to leave, to avoid running into my small, inoffensive mother?' said Basher. He rolled his eyes, but with a smile – like you do with friends.

'I didn't look round the grounds, either. Grass is boring,' said Soph.

Alex googled things like 'How to get blueprints, UK' until they declared that someone should call the local council for Wilbourne Major. Basher was the last to touch his nose.

The lady at the council told Basher that they didn't have anything, because the house was well old and hadn't had any planning permission applications for donkeys', but he should try giving Liz and Joe from the Wilbourne Historical Society a call, because they had all sorts of stuff.

Joe from WHS (Liz was at home, on account of her feet) was very accommodating; he was pleased that anyone was as interested in any bit of Wilbourne's history as he was in all of it. In fact, he said, he *did* have some blueprints for The Cloisters, but they were really very old and might not be much use – but he was happy to send some scans over.

Joe's scans took a while to turn up in Alex's email, because they turned out to be photos he'd taken on a digital camera – most likely whilst standing over the table on a chair, though he had included thoughtful close-ups of some sections. Claire got a bit of a lump in her throat and hoped that Joe had children and grandchildren who appreciated him. The blueprints seemed to be genuine antiques, which Joe almost definitely shouldn't have had, and had probably acquired without asking. They were on thin yellowing paper, looked like they were hand-drawn and showed the house from before the wing existed that the family lived in, so it was a big box with the servants' rooms all in the attic. The grounds were more extensive than Claire had thought.

'Used to have a stable, look,' said Sophie, pointing.

'Cor, that'd be a fucking great place to hide a body,' cooed Claire. 'No horses any more, so nobody goes there – out of view. Classic body stash, right there.'

'Except it doesn't exist in this century,' said Basher.

'A minor detail. Which bits do still exist? Here, look, that must be the ha-ha.'

A curving line bisected the blank expanse of paper that was the lawn. Then there was more lawn, and an area marked as a copse – a lazy kind of kite shape that had some small, inky cloud forms within it. Those, Claire supposed, were the trees she'd seen off in the distance. But tucked behind the top wedge of the copse was a little void of lawn, with a huddle of three buildings in it.

'What does that say? Rains? Ruins?' asked Soph, squinting with her nose almost touching the screen.

'Ruins... Oh!' Claire exclaimed. 'They must be bits of the monastery. Now *that* is a good place for a shallow grave. Away from the house, shielded by the trees there – must be why we didn't see it from the lawn? I bet you that's where the body is.'

'Very ITV teatime,' agreed Soph. 'If the body actually turns out to be there, you'll spaff your pants.'

'C makes a convincing case, Uncle B,' said Alex. 'We should have a look when we're back for the funeral.'

'I'm looking forward to how awkward that's going to be for you, by the way,' said Basher, grinning at Claire. 'I want you to know that.'

'Yeah, yeah, fuck off,' she replied, although quite amicably, and ignoring the faint crackling of an animal impulse somewhere at the back of her brain.

'You should bring the dildo, too, definitely,' said Soph, giggling.

'Wh – oh!' When she'd emptied her bag of her Case Notes, Claire had also displaced the purple dildo. She was surprised to discover that she had been squashing it in her hand like one of those grip-strengthener things.

'You've been doing that the whole time,' said Alex. 'I didn't like to say anything.'

'LOL,' said Soph. 'It's probably the coolest thing you've ever done in your life, you little perv.'

Claire put on *Murder Profile*, which she thought would provide a helpful ambience. She was trying to convince Alex and Basher of its quality, but she was afraid that watching it with them was ruining it for her. Basher pointed out all the practical and legal flaws, and Alex got extremely cross about copaganda. Like, Claire knew they weren't wrong, but that was misunderstanding the appeal of *Murder Profile*. When stern but sexy team leader Smitty responded to a suspect asking for a lawyer by shouting, 'You don't want a lawyer, you want to still be alive in half an hour', was that a violation of rights? Yes. Did it make it harder to see Smitty and the team as the good guys? Also yes. But did it get results? No, because that wasn't actually the murderer, it was a red herring. After a while Claire muted the TV with some savagery and complained that they just didn't get it, but Alex unmuted it and started recording bits of it on their phone, so they could make fun of it in social media posts later.

Basher leaned back, closed his eyes and pinched the bridge of his nose. Claire noticed that he had shaved off all his peach-fuzz beard, which made her a bit sad. She looked at the corners of his lips. His mouth seemed very grave, but the corner looked like he was always close to smiling, or at least smirking a little.

She wondered about him, this quietly sad man who memorized Shakespeare and random facts about fifties comic strips. Who clearly cherished calm and solitude, but had taken in a loud, chaotic teenager who seemed almost his opposite.

'It's like he tries to fade into the background, isn't it?' said Soph, who was watching Claire watching Basher. His hoodie today was the same colour as a sun-faded Royal Mail van. It would have been called Pale Brick or

Dead Salmon on a paint colour chart. 'I wonder if he was always like that, or if he used to be like Alex. Ohmigod, maybe he used to go to all-night ragers and, like, shopped at Cyberdog.'

'How are you?' Claire asked him, on impulse.

'Yeah, have you spoken to your parents or anything?' said Sophie.

'No, not yet. There was a passive-aggressive text from Mum after we left without saying a proper goodbye, though,' said Basher, still keeping his eyes closed. 'And I'm as okay as I ever was. Did Mum or Dad or Figgy or anyone pay you yet, by the way?'

Claire was surprised he'd thought of it. 'No, actually. I wasn't planning to bring it up for a while. For obvious reasons.'

Basher flapped a hand and opened one eye long enough to send a text. 'You have friends in high places now. There. Got on to the patriarchal unit. He'll sort it out soon enough, I expect.'

'Thank you.'

'He's changing the subject. Like, this guy does not want to talk about himself or his feelings *at all*.' Soph leaned forward to wave a cold hand over Basher's face and he shivered. 'How are you really?' she persisted. 'Like, it has been a time of change. And great stress. I know how you're feeling.'

Claire snorted at this, even as she relayed it. In her view, Soph hadn't experienced any change since 2007. Although, in fairness, the change in '07 had been significant.

'I'm fine, really. Mum and Dad are organizing the funeral stuff. It's all fine.'

Claire looked at Soph, who shrugged. Claire thought back to when she met Basher at the house and had mentally compared him to a pigeon. She dug around in her rucksack and retrieved the sharing bag of Starburst that she'd bought at the garage after their flight from The Cloisters. There was still a handful of sweets in it. She nudged Basher and shook the bag in an encouraging way, then stayed very still.

He took one. Excellent.

'How are you feeling about The Case?' she asked.

He shrugged, almost the mirror of Sophie. 'Fine,' he said again. 'I'm still mostly expecting that we'll prove everyone is alive, and nobody is dead.' He looked down and started rubbing the inside of his left palm with his right thumb. 'I hope all that happens is that my dad has to pay a very big tax penalty.' He stopped and looked at Claire, and smiled. 'But in the meantime this has been... I hesitate to say fun exactly, but... not unenjoyable. You are very odd, but I think you know that.'

'Thank you. I, er, like you, too.'

She exchanged a glance with Sophie that communicated the truth they both knew: that therein lay the problem. It had already been days since they'd started hanging out with Basher and Alex, so there wasn't much time left to run out on the clock before something went wrong and they got kicked out. No matter if it was to a gangly fish-worrier or to Alex, Sophie couldn't get too attached because she already knew she wouldn't be

247

staying in Brighton much longer. Quite apart from the sword of Essex hanging over their heads, sending one of Basher and Alex's family down for murder probably wasn't a stable basis for friendship.

Basher's deep, quiet voice broke into her thoughts. 'Huh. Mattie's son David has replied to me,' he said. He sounded genuinely intrigued, as if he hadn't expected anything to come of sending the message at all. 'David said he doesn't want to talk about it and that "you lot have done enough". That's... pointed.'

'Whoa,' said Alex. They sat up. 'That's pretty major, Uncle B. He doesn't say she's alive.'

'He has not said she was mysteriously killed or otherwise spirited into the night, either,' said Basher. 'It is normal to not state the dead-versus-alive status of your parent in small talk.'

'Ask if she's alive, though,' prompted Alex.

'I categorically will *not* do that.'

'It could be just because your family are mostly not very nice and fired Mattie, and accused her of having an affair with your dad,' said Sophie. Basher agreed that this was a solid point and he was pleased to see that someone else was finally thinking sensibly.

'Well, we did maybe dismiss Mattie too quickly before,' said Claire. 'I think we should look into her more.'

'We spoke to her husband. He seemed... sad. Embarrassed,' said Claire. 'Not a killer.'

'Well, as long as he didn't *seem* like a killer, there you are then,' said Basher.

'Yeah, but that guy was definitely hiding something. Maybe they had an argument when he was picking her up or dropping her off at work,' said Sophie, 'and he snapped and hid her body on the property, in a panic.'

'Ooh, okay,' said Alex, getting involved. 'Like, he discovered... she really was having an affair with Grandad!'

'*Sordid* affair.'

'Much as I would like this to be true, for reasons of not being related to a killer, and much as the stats *are* on your side, and much as I appreciate the enthusiasm,' said Basher, in the moderating tone that Claire had come to recognize as the one he used whenever he was about to throw a girder in front of a train of thought, 'we have raised and discounted this idea a ludicrous number of times by this point. And, according to our timeline, Alf would have had to drop Mattie off at work on Saturday morning, give Alex a lift back to the pub and then come back later on in the day, to kill his wife and remove or her hide her body – all without any one of us seeing him there at any time. I think you're going to have to work up some other theories.'

'I am an ideas woman, Basher,' said Claire.

'Yes, I have noticed,' replied Bash, smiling. 'Sadly, to bring a case home we tend to need things like logic and observable facts and rational conclusions, as well.'

'Oh, Claire! What was that business card we found in the office? Remember? What if that was Mattie selling out to Du Lotte?'

Claire had no earthly idea what Soph was talking about. There were several busy minutes while she relayed

Sophie's explanation and then, remembering finding the hotel chain business card in the filing cabinet, she exclaimed, 'Oh!' to herself and started talking over Sophie. Which, to outside observers, was just a woman arguing with herself. In any case, after Alex and Basher had untangled the information, it turned out that Basher couldn't remember where he'd put the card, and that neither of them could remember what the Du Lotte Hotels employee was called, so then they had to endure the agony of navigating a corporate website. But eventually they located Mary Tyler and her phone number.

Claire rang it immediately, which made Basher a bit cross. When Mary Tyler answered, she and Alex and Sophie shrieked like naughty kids making prank calls at a sleepover, and Claire threw the phone at Basher.

'Hello? Hello? Is everything all right?' came the confused voice over the speakerphone.

'Hum. Yes, hello. This is Basher – Sebastian Wellington-Forge. I understand you had an arrangement with Mattie Briggs regarding The Cloisters, my family's home?'

'That depends,' said Mary. Her voice suddenly took on the delicate tones of one who was handling a wild animal and wanted to avoid the teeth. 'Would you like to... come to a similar arrangement?'

Alex, Claire and Sophie were all staring at the phone with eyes like saucers. Somehow, inexplicably, a real clue was happening.

'That depends,' said Basher, matching Mary's tone, 'on the terms of the arrangement.'

Mary sighed very heavily. 'Look, this has been dragging on for fucking ages and, frankly, I'm not sure if that old pile is even worth it, so I'll stop the cloak-and-dagger shit and cut to it. The arrangement was: Mattie told us about tyres to kick that brought down the value of the house, and hence the offer we made. Secret dry rot in the attic, and so on. And in exchange we... showed our appreciation. To a modest extent. But she ran out of useful info before she dropped off the map last year, so I don't know if there's any more you can do for me.'

'Sorry, just a second. So Mattie wasn't trying to force a sale?' asked Basher. 'She didn't get any extra for a sale going through?'

'Of course not. And there's no way she could force a sale anyway. Her name isn't on any of the paperwork. But after talking to Mattie we were able to make an offer that was still attractive to your grandmother, but was equally attractive to our bottom line.'

'And you paid her for this?'

'Now I didn't say that. Call it a cash gift. And not even very much, by the way. I gather Mattie was saving up for something, though. Not that it matters to me now anyway.'

'What do you mean?'

'Well, as I'm sure you know, we were very close to making a deal with your grandmother, but we were recently informed that the estate has now passed to... ah yes, here we are. Clementine, daughter of the deceased. My condolences, by the way. But Clementine has let us know, in no uncertain terms, that a sale will no longer be considered. Under any circumstances. I'm surprised you don't know this already.'

'I am clearly a bit out of the loop,' said Basher.

'I'll say.'

'But, sorry, to circle back – you've not heard from Mattie again?'

'No. She stopped calling around this time last year. I remember because the same awful pumpkin decorations were up in the office. But look, I'm a very busy woman, Sebastian, and I don't want to keep dicking around with this, so how about you call me if your family actually wants to talk, hmm?' Mary Tyler hung up abruptly. Claire imagined her crossing her Louboutins on top of her desk and smoking from a sexy cigarette-holder.

'Wow! I've got to say, I'm fuckin' on Team Mattie for our victim now,' said Sophie. 'Affair with Hugh or not, I bet if Clementine found out that Mattie was passing info to Du Lotte, she'd lose it. I'm saying it was Mrs Wellington-Forge, in the office, with the chicken knife.'

'*Please* stop saying things like that. Let's not jump to any conclusions. I know we have a lot of circumstantial evidence now, but...' said Basher. He was starting to look seriously worried. 'I'll... Look, if I don't hear back from Sami soon, I'll message David, Mattie's son, again, all right? Does that satisfy everyone?'

'Don't worry, Uncle B, we have another potential victim still,' said Alex. They were sorting through Claire's disorganized Case File. The notes had probably made sense to her when she'd written them. 'Look at this obviously crucial theory C worked up. I have a feeling it'll crack The Case wide open.' Alex held up a scrap of paper that said 'K + M TRAFFICKING'.

'Oh, she wrote *that* one after waking herself up in the middle of the night with a really loud snore,' said Soph.

'I don't snore. Did I say what it meant?' asked Claire.

'You said, "Cocaine, Soph, loads of fucking cocaine, it makes sense!" and then fell back asleep,' said Sophie. 'Weirdo. I think your theory was that Michael found out that Monty and Kevin were smuggling loads of coke together, based on the fact that Kevin travels a lot, and Monty and Tris are clearly the type to take titanic amounts of cocaine.'

'Heroic quantities,' agreed Alex. 'Kevin posted another photo on Insta this morning, by the way. "Few cheeky shots in the local bar! #blessed #nomeasures #EyeballPaul". I am glad he is living his best life. Oops, better take this…' Their phone started ringing, so they retreated to their room.

Basher was still leafing through Claire's notes, squinting at her handwriting.

'I still think it would be more helpful if we could, like, interview some of your family,' Claire said. She poked Basher's shoulder to get his attention. 'Even Figgy.'

'Still no,' said Basher, without looking up. 'I am only just about not cross with you for last night. It's lucky Tris won't have the faintest idea what happened. Your notes really are atrocious. You have not properly organized any of your ideas. Have you even considered motives?'

'Yes,' said Claire. She was defensive about her detective work, but also thought it was unfair to blame her for last night when Basher, too, had drunk enough to floor a rugby team. 'As we have already discussed, maybe Kevin was secretly a drug kingpin and murdered Michael, then ran to South America.'

'That is one way to flee a crime scene,' conceded Basher. 'But things are not usually that exotic in real life, I'm afraid.'

'There isn't anything else about Michael that you can remember?'

'Only the breakfast thing. "I'm serious about breakfast, Monty" – that's what he said; or something like that anyway. I wish I could remember. But he mostly kept himself to himself. Sensible man.'

'Like me, right?' said Sophie.

'Yes, of course. My compatriot in reason.'

The Entente Sensible was weakened by the reappearance of Alex, who looked positively incandescent with excitement. They clearly had something thrilling to say, but couldn't choose between saying it immediately and withholding it, for the drama.

'He's alive!' they exclaimed, sort of plumping for both at once.

'Who is?' asked Basher, trying to still sound disinterested.

'Michael!'

'How does your mum know Michael's alive?'

'That wasn't my mum, stupid. She's fine, by the way,

although it's been weirdly difficult to get hold of her. No, Helen told me.'

'Who the fuck is Helen?' asked Sophie.

'The office manager at Dad's firm. Remember I said I called Dad's office, about visiting? Helen called me back just now to arrange it – but *she let slip* that Michael was still on secondment there until a couple of weeks ago, when he left without any warning! And apparently he left a load of stuff behind. Let's go and look through it all.'

'*Ohmigod*, yes! Industrial espionage. Let's do it,' said Soph. The dead girl looked suddenly very lively and excitable.

'I... I guess I could try and get in touch with him? Michael's never met me, so he won't be suspicious,' said Claire. 'And there's all the stuff he left in the office, right?'

'All right, that is enough,' said Basher, abruptly standing up. 'I can allow Alex to suggest a lot of wild ideas, but as a notionally responsible uncle, I have to draw the line at things like actual crime. I may not be a police officer any more, but pawing through personal belongings, or any business files that you can find in a privately owned office, sounds suspiciously felonious to me. And if Michael is alive, there's no need to investigate his disappearance, is there? The plan is... the plan is that we wait for Sami to get back to me, before we do anything stupid. Right? Yes?'

He stalked into the kitchen and there were sounds of him rooting around in the fridge. Claire heard him say, 'I thought I had some ham in here...' before Basher turned on the roaring kettle.

He reappeared suddenly and pointed a butter knife at them, for emphasis, as he spoke. 'Do not – and I cannot stress this enough – get on a train to London, try to interview Michael or break into Monty's office. I am very serious about this.'

13

The Gang Gets on a
Train to London

'Here,' said Alex, sliding a little plastic packet across the table. Claire picked it up. It had a blocky Bluetooth earpiece in it, of the kind beloved by middle-aged men driving Land Rovers around the M25.

'Thank you,' she said. She was confused, although she didn't say it. Like most normal people, Claire viewed phone calls the same way she viewed flavoured gin: with suspicion, and as a last resort only. The whole point of texting was not having to call people. Soph had liked calls, though, and she used to call Claire and immediately hang up, so Claire had to phone back and Sophie didn't use up any credit.

'I thought if you wore it, people would think you were on the phone with someone. Rather than talking to yourself. You know, with the "Sophie says" stuff all the time,'

Alex explained.

'Oh. That's... actually a very good idea.' Claire struggled to tear the vacuform prison open.

'Alex talks to me out loud,' said Sophie. 'They don't get embarrassed.'

Claire did not repeat this.

'You can pay me back whenever,' said Alex.

Claire chose to strategically ignore this. In fairness, Alex had been letting her bum cigarettes off them for days.

It was Friday. The three of them – Claire, Sophie and Alex – were seated on a mainline train that was still on the platform at Brighton, owing to a points failure. There were often points failures on the Brighton mainline, but today's were a special annoyance because the line had been out of use for almost all of September for essential maintenance, notably to the points.

Claire found that, while to start with she'd seen Alex as a raven or a crow, as time went on she was increasingly comparing Alex to sweets. They were in cream jeans and a pink blouse, so it looked as if an incredibly cool drumstick lolly was wedged in one corner, against the train window, in order to make full use of the socket. Sophie was next to them.

They were going to London for exactly the reasons Basher had told them they were not allowed to. More pressing for Claire was that this whole thing was originally meant to be a weekend job, over by Sunday. A surprise murder investigation had now dragged it out for five more days, so Claire was at the 'wearing a used pair of pants inside out' stage of travel discomfort. She had also been hauling around a massive Bible, bell and a candlestick wherever she went, which was quite inconvenient.

It had taken a day for the three of them to decide on their forbidden plan and then carry it out. Luckily, Basher would be at work for most of today, so it would take ages for him to realize they were gone. After all, as Alex had reasoned, they were both adults who could make their own decisions and were doing nothing wrong by going to London (which did not exactly chime with going in secret, but let's not think about that too closely).

Thursday, as the day before their daring heist, had accordingly been spent on fun. They'd passed the time walking to Hove and looking for new clothes for Claire, who had loved the outfits Alex picked out, but then felt self-conscious in them and had returned to the comfort of her faded jeans.

There had, however, been one anxiety-inducing incident when they went to the pier in the evening, with Sami and her husband and children. Sami had confirmed that no, there were no Missing Persons reports on anyone involved, but that was not the source of the anxiety. The weather had been blustery and clear, and the lights of the boardwalk reflected off the water. The sea air blew through Claire to her very core, carrying the smell of candy floss and hot, fresh doughnuts. Sophie ran back and forth after Sami's kids, watching them, and watching chips and waffles being fried. Halloween decorations were still up everywhere.

Claire had gone out for a cigarette, coughing into

the wind as it snatched the smoke away, while everyone else was in the arcade yelling at the 2p fall coin-pusher machines. Sami came out and stood next to her. She looked out across the waves and did not turn her head to look at Claire.

'I looked you up,' she said.

Claire's chest burned. She began to shiver as adrenaline suddenly coursed through her. She looked around, but Soph was nowhere to be seen. Claire said, 'Er...' and Sami didn't say anything for a long time.

'You know,' she replied suddenly. 'I get pretty sick of Basher's shit sometimes.'

'Er... what d'you mean?'

'Oh, you know. This constant fucking "Woe is me, misery, misery" shit, but at the same time as "Basher knows best". I would have thought it was pretty difficult to have an inferiority complex at the same time as a superiority complex, but then he is also an over-achiever... Did he tell you why he quit his job?'

'Uh, yeah. He said, like, he couldn't be part of the system any more and—'

'Thought so. See, that's what *I* said.' Sami didn't sound angry. She sounded very tired. '*I* wanted to quit, and *I* hated being part of that system, but apparently I said it often enough that he thought it was his idea. And I *can't* quit because I have two kids and a mortgage, and Brighton won't support as many private detectives or security consultants as it does drag brunches. Basher didn't even *ask* me if I wanted to leave, too. If his leaving would affect my plans. Didn't even say he was going.' She leaned on the railing, the wind whipping her hair across her face. 'I won't tell Basher and Alex about you yet,' she said, after another long wait. 'But you should. I'll give you another day or so, but you need to say something.'

'Thank you,' said Claire. But she said it so quietly, as Sami walked away, that she thought it might have disappeared into the air, along with her fag smoke.

She hadn't told Sophie about the conversation. She wasn't sure why, except that Sophie was happy at the moment, and Claire knew, deep down, that she wasn't going to say anything to Basher and Alex anyway, because if you didn't think about something, it was sort of like it wasn't happening.

She sighed heavily now, remembering it all, and had a coughing fit. It sounded like she was hacking up both of her own lungs, and possibly someone else's as well. Alex reached over with their long, graceful arms to alternate rubbing her on the back with smacking her between her shoulder blades, like a parent attending to a toddler who'd tried to swallow an entire Twix in one go.

'God, are you still feeling rough from the other night, C? I thought Uncle B was exaggerating about how bad hangovers are, when you're ancient,' they observed. 'I suppose being a smoker doesn't help. Maybe I should quit. Maybe *you* should quit. And go home and get into bed.'

Claire considered this. She and Sophie lived in a poky flat above a twenty-four-hour newsagent, and whenever it rained (so approximately eight to ten months of every year) the roof started leaking near the foot of her bed. This meant the flat was also damp, but Sophie kept telling her that it was black mould and not damp, and that pretty soon they would *both* be dead, and Claire would be found frozen in bed like Jack Nicholson at the end of *The Shining*, half eaten by cats and/or rats.

'I am not sure,' she replied, when she got her breath back, 'if that would help.'

'Also,' said Sophie, with some indignation, 'I would get really fucking bored.'

Claire looked out of the window.

'When I was little,' she said, 'I used to sit in trains and cars looking out of the window and imagine we were keeping a few feet ahead of a catastrophe – like a tornado or a fucking, giant saw blade. And it was ripping everything up behind us, but we stayed just ahead of it.'

'Really?' said Alex. 'Me too. Huh. Cool.'

'You never told me that,' said Soph. 'You massive weirdo.' She sounded hurt.

'We don't have to tell each other everything, you know,' replied Claire.

It was only about an hour before Claire was looking down at the great grey sweep of the Thames and the Chelsea suspension bridge, which looked so pretty lit up at night. She was of the considered opinion – having never lived anywhere else – that London was the greatest city in the world. She contained multitudes. In the sunshine, she glowed. Even the grime and pigeon shit and piss-soaked alleys glowed. Today was another grey day spattered with rain and whipped by wind, and the whole town felt grey and glowering, like the city was hunched over herself. Waiting. Biding her time. Claire always thought of London as a she. Very Freudian, probably.

She led Alex through Victoria Station with the air of a tour guide at the National Gallery, with Soph mooching along behind with a slight smirk on her face, like a teenager who was bored by the tour guide at the National Gallery.

'Just follow me on the Tube; it's a bit overwhelming at first, but it's actually *reeeally* fucking simple – you only need to not let the crowds get to you. And have your ticket ready, because otherwise everyone will tut at you at the barriers—'

She stopped when she realized that Alex was looking at her strangely.

'Yeah... You realize I grew up here, right, C? Like, I am from London?'

'Er...'

Sophie started laughing. 'Yikes. Felt that one!'

Monty and Tristan's office was near St Paul's, and Soph was a bit sad they didn't get to walk down Fleet Street. She liked the strange, narrow buildings – the pubs that were five storeys tall, but fifteen feet wide.

'The deados down there are fun to talk to as well,' she added, looking wistfully in that direction. '*Ohmigod*, trying to explain this century to a drunk journalist who's been dead, like, hundreds of years? Suddenly things don't seem so bad. They're always like "But what of the Poor Laws!" or "What became of the *Whigs*?" or whatever.'

The office had the sleek, early noughties look of frosted glass and chrome, but someone had made recent efforts to incorporate the current trend for exposed brick, coffee table books about design and funky pot plants. The complimentary fruit juice said, 'We've heard of Silicon Valley'; the small inflatable ball pit in the corner added, 'But we did not really understand what we heard.'

Alex breezed everyone through reception with a cheery wave to the woman behind the counter and into a lift. They had a security pass, so they could visit their dad, although they claimed they never really used it.

'Just leave the talking to me, okay?' they said, tapping away at their phone still. 'Dad and Uncle T probably aren't even here.'

Soph whistled when they stepped out of the lift. The place was full of grey desks staffed by identikit law boys exactly like Tristan, working away on computers and exchanging paper files, and occasionally cracking the air of industrious quiet with a braying laugh.

'Drop an allergy pill, C – this place must really be setting off your eat-the-rich glands.'

'Jesus,' said Claire. 'It's like a *Where's Wally?* book of cunts.' Alex let out a single loud 'HA!' and then clapped their hand over their mouth, as every eye in the room swivelled towards them.

Two of them belonged to a woman in her thirties and were behind some extremely fifties cat's-eye glasses. She bustled over. 'Hi, Alex! We weren't expecting you to bring anyone.' It was a statement, not a question.

'Hi, Helen. I'm in town visiting my friend Claire, and it seemed rude to leave her outside. Just wondering if Dad or Uncle T might be around for lunch later.'

Helen gave a bright smile. 'Oh, *fun*. Come over to my desk and I'll check your dad's schedule.'

'Oh, H, I was meaning to ask,' Alex said, as if it hardly mattered at all, 'do you have a number for that Michael, the accountant guy we talked about the other day? He seemed cool – I wanted to ask him some stuff about doing taxes as a freelancer.'

'Uh, funny you should ask, I was just thinking about the box of his stuff I have in that meeting room. I have *no* idea what to do with it,' Helen replied, pulling up a calendar on her computer. 'He left without saying anything or even packing up his desk, did I tell you that?'

'Wow, *rude*,' said Alex, making eyes at Claire.

'Say you need a slash, genius,' said Sophie.

'Er, Alex, do you know where the toilets are?'

Alex waved vaguely down a corridor and continued to distract Helen with banal chit-chat. Claire and Sophie were able to duck into the conference room quite easily. The room clearly wasn't used much, and there were a few cardboard boxes stacked in different corners.

'It's this one,' said Sophie, tippy-tapping on her feet next to one box, like a cat waiting for food. She couldn't properly look inside until Claire opened it for her.

'How d'you know?' said Claire.

'It says "Michael's stuff" on the top. You are the world's worst fucking detective. I'm serious.'

Michael hadn't actually left that much. There was a stress ball and a fake cactus, a mouse mat and a bunch of notepads – yellow legal paper ones that opened upwards instead of sideways.

'If he was on secondment, this wasn't really *his* office,' said Sophie. 'I bet he didn't bring a lot of desk stuff with him. I wouldn't be arsed, would you?'

Claire shook her head and flipped through a couple of the notepads. They were blank new ones. All unused. 'It's a bust. Again,' she said. She felt like a deflated balloon. 'I'm starting to think maybe nothing did happen after all.'

'Maybe,' said Soph. She shrugged.

'You serious?' hissed Claire. 'You're the one who was all "Do this for me! Do it for Nana!" about it. You convinced me!'

'Sure. It's fun to pretend stuff happens. Sometimes it doesn't.'

'Unbelievable!' Claire slid down onto the floor and found she was blinking very quickly and trying not to cry. Stories in real life are not as neat as they are on television. Living was hard. Sometimes Soph forgot that.

'Hey, don't worry!' said Soph. 'I still think something's up. That ghost in the library was definitely real, anyway.'

Claire nodded. She half-heartedly flipped through the pages of another notepad. A loose sheet fell out of the back of it.

She grabbed it and quickly got to her feet. She glanced at it and saw it was a single printed-off email, which definitely felt like a clue. She stuffed it into her backpack, which was being forced more and more to play the role of Mary Poppins's infinite carpet bag, and then hastily left the room again, anxious not to be caught. She was not, unfortunately, as confident during searches as the *Murder Profile* crew were. Somehow she thought that if she tried the 'I can always come back with a search warrant!' line, it would not be as convincing.

'Come the fuck on,' moaned Sophie, 'you barely did anything there – we can't go yet. Look, this says it's Monty's office. Let's go in.'

Claire hesitated, jiggling her leg like a dog that needs a piss.

'Ohmigod, Claire, you watch that stupid show all the time, but when it actually comes down to it, you won't do any crime-solving at all. Put up or fuck up, come o-o-on.'

Claire relented, looking quickly around and trying the door. To her disappointment, it was open. Soph was delighted, and whooped as Claire slid inside, pointing out that, really, the worst that could happen was that she'd be chucked out – it wasn't like she was in danger of being murdered or anything. Although, er, come to think of it...

Claire's heart started to pound. She genuinely had no excuse or reason to be in there. It was the office at The Cloisters, all over again. She started to have visions of Clem bursting through the door wielding a still-greasy kitchen knife.

Monty's office was quite utilitarian. It had a glass desk, glass shelves and a set of spangly new tumbler glasses next to a decanter. Glass was the overall theme. Claire was tempted to sit in the chair behind the desk and pretend she had an entirely different life. She sometimes secretly wondered if she could ever have been that sort of person: do this, sue that person, rabble-rabble-rabble!

She swiftly decided that there'd be no point trying the computer, since Monty evidently had a firmer grasp of digital security than his dad did, so she started to rifle through the paperwork in his desk organizer.

'Look at this,' said Soph. She was gazing at an open folder on the side table (glass). 'It's Nana's will! She left everything to Bash! But there's a sticky note on it listing, like, possible ways to challenge it. I think they're trying to claw it back from him. Fuck, he probably doesn't even know.'

'Yeah, remember they told Du Lotte that Clementine inherited, too, so they're lying to everyone. God, what a bunch of... of...' Claire, growing more and more angry on Basher's behalf, the longer she thought about it, couldn't find a word that fully expressed her contempt for Basher and Alex's extended family. 'What a bunch of *losers*.'

'Tell 'em how you really feel, C,' said Sophie.

'Well, they are – they're just terrible at being people. Who does that? Who tries to snatch back an inheritance from their own son? I am honestly so surprised Nana wasn't murdered,' said Claire. 'Genuinely seems more likely than natural causes. *Oooh!*'

She had come across a letter notifying Monty that Tuppence had applied for a divorce. This seemed more like salacious gossip than detective work, but it did give Claire no small amount of evil satisfaction. Yeah, Tuppence. Fuck that guy. Sisters are doing it for themselves.

'Huh. You know if I were Monty, I'd give Tuppence the divorce as quickly as possible, *before* I contested the will, because if I managed to get anything out of it, I wouldn't want to then have to share it with my ex,' said Sophie, looking over Claire's shoulder.

'Jesus! We're lucky you aren't Monty. Sometimes the way your mind works is quite frightening. Anyway he won't do that, because he's clearly way too much of a controlling dickhead to not object to the divorce.'

They suddenly heard Alex's voice approaching, saying, 'I thought you'd be pleased to see me, *Dad*!' at high volume – practically shouting, in fact. Claire immediately flew into a high panic. She was trapped like a rat and began uselessly circling the desk. Hiding under it surely wouldn't work, would it? No, stupid idea; it was see-through.

'The window – stand by the window!' hissed Sophie. 'Get as far away from any *stuff* as possible.'

Claire hopped over and managed to be looking out at the view as Monty entered, flanked by Alex, Helen and his usual hype-man, Tristan, who was nervously vibrating as if he'd just done a line, but was also afraid he was about to find out it had been cut with something unpleasant.

'Well,' said Monty, as chilly as Sophie, 'this doesn't seem at all suspicious.'

'He's got us there,' said Sophie, clearly amused. 'How are the gang going to get out of this one? Because I think the answer will be "Flail and say 'er' a lot" like a big fanny. But let's see.'

Claire took a deep, shaky breath in and tried to imagine what Smitty and the *Murder Profile* team would do: act with confidence, lie and probably lightly brutalize the suspect.

'Suspicious in what way exactly?' she said, sounding very calm, despite the fact that she was pretty sure even the soles of her feet were sweating. 'I'm concerned about the matter of my pay for this past weekend, since I still haven't heard from anyone. I thought it was perfectly acceptable to wait in the fuc— Ahem, in the office of a lawyer on business premises. I'm sorry if I am incorrect about that. What else do you imagine I would be doing?'

Claire wasn't sure where it had come from, or why she'd sounded increasingly formal as she spoke, but she was pretty happy with that.

'Wow! Okay. That was great – good for you, weirdo, I take it all back. I think he actually is going to kill you now, but it'll be worth it,' said Sophie.

Monty narrowed his eyes.

'I am sure I don't know,' he said, after a length of time during which Claire was sure the seas froze and melted again, mountains crumbled and stars went supernova in the vastness of space. 'You will be paid. It hasn't even been a week yet. Rest assured, we settle debts with even the most minor of employees. I would like you to leave, please.'

Claire suppressed a shiver, and realized that she definitely didn't have another performance like that in her, and that Monty in terror mode was the next-closest thing she had experienced to Clementine with the kitchen knife.

They trooped out. It felt very much like Claire was leaving the headmaster's office after getting detention, and she felt a flush rising to her cheeks.

'He's not wearing that gaudy tie-pin any more,' commented Sophie. 'Maybe he's having to liquidate some assets...'

'I hear you were asking about Michael, Alex,' said Monty, walking and talking them through the office in a really shit version of *The West Wing*. 'He is not a very good accountant, and we are no longer working with his company. We can put you in touch with a better one. Helen, please compile a list.'

Helen nodded and appeared to start doing so immediately, on a sleek Samsung phone. Sophie was very interested by this. 'Ask if that's the standard company issue,' she said quickly.

Claire did so, and Helen answered in the affirmative, and Monty looked at Claire with even deeper suspicion.

'I thought Michael was quite nice,' said Alex, who was very unperturbed by Monty's potential rage.

'Please, let's keep going, shall we? I'm going to put your strange behaviour down to grief, in this instance,' said Monty.

'So, Alex, yah, we should totally go out, if you're in town tonight,' said Tristan, who clearly now saw himself as the funcle – or, at least, wanted to. 'There's this really cool bar that me and some of the boys go to, that does, like, massive trays of themed shots?'

'Sounds good, Uncle T,' said Alex, in a kind yet massively condescending tone of voice that Tristan seemed not to notice. 'I don't know what my plans are. I'll let you know, okay?'

'Yeah. Cool! So, like, you know if you do shots into your eye, it gets you drunk quicker?'

'You've said that before, Uncle T, and I really don't think it's true.'

'That is an incredibly stupid thing to say to my child, Tristan. Alex, we will speak later,' said Monty as he deposited them back in the lift. 'And you...' the icy-blue eye of Sauron fixed itself on Claire, 'it would not affect my life in any way, whatsoever, if I never saw or heard from you ever again.'

Claire waited until the doors had closed and the lift had started moving before leaning heavily against a wall. 'Jesus. Christ. Fuck. Alex, your dad is terrifying.'

Sophie was crouching on the floor with her hands on the back of her head, as if she was in a plane that was about to crash.

'Fucking hell. That was almost as bad as the chicken thing,' she moaned.

'He gets it from Granny, but I've had a lifetime of practice with it,' said Alex, back to tapping on their phone straight away. 'All bark and no bite,' they added.

'That was my second field operation, though,' added

Claire, brightening up a bit. 'How did I do? I think I was better that time.'

'Aw, you did really well,' said Alex, looking up. 'Caught my loud and obvious signal and everything.'

Claire beamed.

Summing Up

'What do we do now?' asked Claire, as they huddled on the windy street outside.

'You're asking me? You're the grown up, C,' Alex pointed out. 'Ha! Only joking. Your face! At what point are you going to start being comfortable with any amount of responsibility whatsoever? Don't worry, I've arranged to meet Mum for lunch at the National Theatre. Bit early, but we can mooch over to the South Bank now.'

'Oh, sure, that'll be cheap,' said Soph. 'You enjoying pretending you can afford to grab lunch at the Nash, babes?'

Claire did like the National Theatre, though. A big, raw concrete fuck-off of a building: a pile of rectangles and layers that, when viewed from some angles, looked very persuasively like a dominant cruise ship that was trying to top every boat on the Thames. And inside its echoing heart, words came alive.

She had seen a play there in person once in her life, with her school. She remembered feeling the huge, sucking space in front of her, and how amplified the small, personal sounds of the audience were. How a tiny cough echoed around the vast auditorium, and how she had been frozen in fear, not wanting to make a sound because someone would hear and they would know – they would know it was her who had made it and she'd be told off. And then the stage lights went up and she saw how magic was somehow real. She saw the floor lift up and turn and become a room within a room, and she saw paper animals come alive, and a hole cut in the sky.

How could a building be so ugly and so beautiful at the same time? How could it produce the impossible? How could people be other people?

But as she got older, the National Theatre had started to remind Claire more of the sarcophagus over the Chernobyl reactor, put there to stop the radiation from leaking out too much. She started to suspect that some types of theatre people wanted to stop the magic inside the National getting out, in case ordinary people discovered it worked for them as well. The prohibitive cost of most theatre tickets helped, too, of course.

It started to rain as they arrived, so they huddled at a table inside the little canteen and Claire felt the great weight of the building on top of them, and wondered if they'd be able to make it out and far enough away if it started to collapse.

'It's good we're meeting your mum,' she said to Alex. 'She could be just the neutral witness we need to bust The Case wide open. In *Murder Profile* there's always, like, some urchin hiding up a chimney or in a bookshelf who knows who the killer is the whole time, but only gets found in the last ten minutes.'

The Wellington-Forges at large seemed to treat Tuppence as less like a member of the family and more like a trusted servant, ever present, yet always unseen and unnoticed. It would actually form the basis for a pretty good motive for murder. Except that, based on the TV she watched, the choice of victim didn't make sense: Claire would have expected Tuppence to suddenly snap and rage-kill her husband and in-laws, turning them into mannequins that she arranged around the dinner table – and possibly later into stringed puppets to act out the sort of loving family meal that she had always wanted. Divorce was probably a safer option. Claire wondered if she should tell Alex. It was a bit of a guilty secret to have, but it seemed like the sort of thing that was supposed to come from your parents. If she hadn't been snooping around Monty's office, she wouldn't have known anyway.

'Did you say *in* a bookshelf?' said Sophie, breaking through her thoughts. Luckily Claire didn't need to defend herself, because Alex got a phone call.

'Yello... I'm fine. Yeah. Yeah, I am. Really? Okay.' They held the phone out to Claire. 'It's for you.'

'Er... hello?' said Claire, looking to Sophie for reassurance.

'Don't look at me,' she replied.

'Ahoy!'

'Oh. Hello, Hugh.'

'Yes, indeedy. M'boy Basher said you needed paying, and we'd normally do thirty-day terms and so on, but, well, friend of the family and all that. So it should have come through. It's from a company account.'

'Right, well. Er, thank you, Hugh.' He sounded about as awkward as she did. It felt very much like a conversation neither of them wanted to have, which prompted the question: why were they having it?

'Yes and er...' Claire could swear she could hear someone whispering in the background. 'Yes, and we hope you do stay a *friend*,' said Hugh, reading from *The Ladybird Book of First Veiled Threats*.

'Yes. Me, too.'

'Jolly good. So we've sent a little extra to make sure – to *en*sure your discretion.'

'About what?' said Claire quickly.

'Er, everything. Anything. Whatever you feel might need it,' said Hugh, casting a wide and desperate net. Claire could hear his perspiration down the phone.

'Right, yes. Of course.'

'Because m'boy Monty mentioned you'd just been by with Alex. And we felt that maybe you'd got hold of the wrong end of the old stick.'

'Oh, I'm sure I haven't,' said Claire cheerfully. 'Don't worry.'

'Yes and... *I* am *doing it* – and, needless to say, it would probably be inappropriate for you to come to the funeral. Friends don't always have to see each other, to stay friendly.'

'Of course, Hugh,' said Claire, who was honestly starting to feel sorry for him. 'Don't let it trouble you. Thank you and goodbye. And my condolences again.'

She checked the banking app on her phone as soon as she hung up. She had indeed received a payment from a generic business name that she didn't recognize. She scribbled the name, Arrowhead Beacon, on the back of her train ticket and made a mental note to add it to her Case Notes later. Soph, looking over her shoulder at the amount, whistled.

'That's... way too much. Even with how much you inflated your price for them.'

Alex was looking at her curiously – expecting her to explain the call, she realized. 'It was nothing really,' she said. 'Hugh wanted to make sure the money came through, and asked me not to come to Nana's funeral.'

'Ha! Classic us,' said Alex.

Claire chewed her lip. She didn't feel good keeping more secrets from Basher and Alex, even though it was because neither Soph nor Claire wanted to upset their newest, bestest friends with news about how criminal or awful their family was. She still hadn't decided whether they should say anything about Nana's will or Tuppence's yearning for freedom. She would have felt awkward having lunch with Tuppence even without knowing she was keeping the divorce a secret. Claire was letting her feelings compromise her unimpeachableness as a detective, which was always a bad sign. Next thing you knew, she'd be in danger of forgetting which side she was on.

Tuppence arrived, accompanied by the faint scent of lilies and a general air of capitulation. She looked pleased to see her child, and had pink cheeks and sensible mum-jeans. She was adept at nice mum-pleasantries and talked about how she didn't have much to do at home, but everyone was very busy with the funeral at The Cloisters, and how she didn't like to be a bother, and so on and so forth.

'Oh, I thought you'd stayed down there,' said Alex. 'I keep not getting through when I call you. And I texted you a couple of times, but they didn't send until yesterday. I assumed you didn't have signal.'

'That's odd,' said Tuppence brightly. 'No, just been rattling about at home all alone, I'm afraid.'

Claire cleared her throat. 'Do you remember Nana's birthday last year?' she asked.

Tuppence replied in the affirmative. Her brief description of the dinner tallied pretty closely with everyone else's.

'It sounds like you were gone for a while, making gravy.'

Claire might have imagined it, but she thought Tuppence went the slightest shade pinker. 'Was I?' she said absent-mindedly. 'I suppose I was. I think it must have taken me quite a while to find the instant gravy, you know. Clem does make a big thing out of having it at the back of a shelf.'

'And what time did you go to bed that night?' Claire was getting businesslike. She was quite enjoying herself. Alex was staying uncharacteristically quiet.

'Oh, gosh. I don't remember, I'm afraid. I think we stayed up in the kitchen for a little while, didn't we, Alex? There was some fuss about Tristan ruining a suit, but he didn't come back in through the kitchen, I don't think. I wasn't up too late. I remember I wasn't staying in the same room as Monty because he was always up working. Sorry, not very helpful, I expect.'

Tuppence's genuine desire to be helpful was matched only by how terminally incurious she was. Not only did she not seem to care why Claire was asking this, but she also hadn't observed anything she considered odd during the entire weekend. She was very apologetic about this, as she was about everything.

Sophie clearly found her quite boring. She had propped her head in her hand and was staring right through Tuppence, not really paying attention. Soph sighed and it blew in Tuppence's face, in response to which Tuppence shivered and fished a carefully folded cardigan out of her massive standard-issue mum shoulder bag.

'Chilly in here, isn't it?' she said, shrugging it on.

The cardigan had a transformative effect on Sophie, who immediately sat up and stared. 'Oh no,' she said. 'The buttons. Look at the fucking buttons! They're little crystal ones. Ugh, there's even one missing. Christ, I can't take much more of this.'

'Er... Weird question, Tuppence, but do you go in the library at The Cloisters very often?'

'No, I don't. It's a bit spooky in there, if you ask me.'

'What about the priest-hole?'

'No,' said Tuppence, right away. Almost too quickly, Claire thought. 'I wouldn't have any reason to. It would be a bit silly to go standing around in a little box, wouldn't it?'

'Oh, well. It's nothing really. I just found this in there and it looks like one of yours,' said Claire, producing the treasured button, which had stood up so well to interrogation. But it had finally broken and given up its boss, so she could probably hand it back.

'Oh, how funny,' Tuppence said. Claire wasn't imagining it: Tuppence had definitely gone at least two shades pinker. 'It must have rolled in there or something. I can sew it back on now at least. Thank you.' She took it and wrapped it in a handkerchief, which was exactly the sort of thing she would have on hand, to wrap errant buttons in.

Tuppence pulled her sleeves over her hands and got up to pay. She invited Claire to have dinner over at theirs, and Alex brightened at the suggestion. 'Fancy a trip to our place in Richmond, C?'

'Full offence,' said Claire, while Tuppence was at the till, 'but that is fucking miles away.'

'It's not that far,' said Alex. 'I mean, we came here from Brighton.'

'Yeah, and it'll take almost the same amount of time to get to Richmond! Richmond *is* miles away, even by London-to-Greater-London standards.'

Those standards never really made sense in the context of anywhere else, Claire thought. On a night out in London she had heard people say things like, 'Yeah, Stratford is dead, mate, but a friend of a friend is apparently at a great house-party in Battersea', which in travel terms was almost like someone in London complaining that England was boring, but they'd heard there was a great party currently happening in Dublin.

'Well, look,' Claire said, 'if we're going to Richmond, I definitely need to go back to my flat first and get a clean pair of pants.'

'Fair enough, grubby knickers,' said Alex.

'If Monty catches you at his house, it is one hundred per cent chicken-soup time,' said Soph. 'This is a terrible idea.'

Claire mulled over the potential of being turned into a family meal as they got on the Tube to her flat in Brixton. It was an idea she kept coming back to, so perhaps that really was the key to the whole thing: The Cloisters was actually a front for an elite club of cannibals. It wouldn't be that surprising.

'You know what,' she mumbled, once they had arrived, 'don't come up. It's not very big.'

'Don't be silly, C,' said Alex, pushing their way past.

The sight of Alex standing politely in the kitchen-cum-all-purpose-living-area, which, when you allowed for furniture, was barely large enough for all three of them to fit in at once, without Sophie literally standing in someone, made Claire oscillate between shame and defiance. She shouldn't have let them come up, damn it. But then again, what of it? This was how normal people had to live! London was probably loads of fun if you were rich and came from Richmond, and didn't have to think twice about having extra cheese on your plain pasta as a treat. Fuck them!

She realized she had been standing stock-still, in silence, for some time. Sophie was looking at her. Claire found herself wishing she could curl up under the duvet and sleep for an entire day. She was tired in her very bones, a tiredness she could not shake, and she wanted to be alone to think and exhale.

She couldn't shake the feeling that the answer to The Case – which would, of course, solve all her problems – was staring her in the face; that she'd heard or seen something that was important, and if she got hold of the last piece, they could put it all together. Like getting the centre square on *Catchphrase*. Although Soph was better at that, too.

She escaped to her room, where, instead of collapsing on her bed, she threw the old clothes in her bag onto the washing heap, avoided looking in the mirror and had a quick sink-wash.

When she stepped back into the living area, Alex had already become characteristically at ease and appeared to be looking for teabags. Claire pushed the second-hand Ikea coffee table (which doubled as her dining table and desk) up to the wall to try and make more room, and also so that she could discreetly sweep some old crumbs off it and onto the floor. Unfortunately there was no way to dispel the general gloom, since the only window opened onto an alley and was close to the wall of the building next door. The curtains could never really be opened far enough. Luckily, Alex had already got into the habit of carrying extra jumpers or fuzzy scarves, for times when they would be in enclosed spaces with Sophie.

Alex, after some furious texting and a phone call to their mum, declared they had changed their mind and wanted to go out in Brixton with some friends. Claire hesitated at this, but Alex was something of an unstoppable force.

'It'll be fun! Come on, seize the moment. Live in the now!'

'Some of us don't even live in the anything,' grumbled Sophie. 'I told you, it's rubbish watching you all get drunk.'

'Don't be like that. I'll talk to you, I promise.'

Before Claire could stop them, Alex had rifled through her wardrobe to produce tights and a bright red dress that she hadn't worn in years, held it up against her with a critical eye, declared that it would do and waited while Claire got changed. Suddenly she found herself stumbling from bar to house-party and back again. Claire started the night feeling like a haggard old woman trying to pretend she was young – the sort of person who would force her daughter to take her out and screech, 'They think we're sisters!' at people – and ended it feeling like she was back at university. This was probably not a good thing.

If it hadn't been for Sophie – perennially sober and once again furious, because while Alex sporadically remembered to talk to her, Claire kept forgetting to relay the conversation – Claire would probably have forgotten how to get home.

Alex fell into bed when they got back and looked at their phone. 'Ha-ha-ha,' they mumbled. 'Million missed calls from Uncle B. Ha-ha! Sh'up.'

Claire went to the bathroom and was heartily sick in the toilet. Alex was a bad influence.

She woke up the next morning half curled in the foetal position on the sofa. Consciousness came to her like a brick hitting an egg. Someone was hammering on the door of her flat.

'Oh God. Eurgh,' said Claire. She wasn't used to being hungover, and certainly not twice in quick succession. She couldn't be sure she wasn't actually the butt of a smoked cigarette that had been stubbed out on top of a bin, and then found by a disgruntled fairy godmother and cursed to live as a human. She crawled to the toilet and was sick again, which made her feel a bit better. Sophie watched her without any trace of sympathy.

Alex stumbled in, their hair plastered to their face on one side and sticking straight in the air on the other. Claire realized that they would be fine almost as soon as they had some coffee.

'Soph, please go and see who that is, before I die of noise.'

Sophie went out to listen at the door. She came back into the room and looked at Claire, and Claire knew at once – because she knew Sophie's face like she knew her own

– that Soph was worried. Her eyes did not sparkle. They were as dark and dull as pebbles, as cold as flint buried in a field and left undisturbed by the metal teeth of the plough.

'It's Basher. He's, like, well angry. Furious,' said Soph, in a leaden voice.

Claire's stomach dropped. Sophie was the constant by which she set her own mood. When she said, 'I don't like this, Claire', then Claire did not like it, either.

She opened the door, and Basher brushed past her without a word. 'Hello?' she said. 'What are you doing here? And how did you know where I live?'

'Your address is on the invoice you sent my parents,' Basher replied in a monotone. He didn't turn round. 'Alex? Are you all right?'

Alex was in the kitchen area. They turned and handed Claire a mug of tea. 'Wotcher, Uncle B. Cuppa?'

Claire perched gingerly on the coffee table, cupping her mug in both hands like a shield. Sophie stood in the corner. Alex threw themself down on the sofa, taking up its entire length and groaning theatrically. And Basher was standing in front of them, framed in the gap that marked the border between the watching-television area and the preparing-food area of the room. For the first time Claire saw him as he must have looked as a police detective. Basher did not speak, but began pacing back and forth, breathing hard, like he'd just finished a sprint.

'So-o-o… what are you doing in town, Uncle B?' asked Alex, flashing a winning smile. They were trying to disarm him.

'You know exactly why I am here,' he growled. 'What on earth did you think you were doing? You vanished – without a call, without a text, *nothing*. Disappeared with this... this fucking charlatan that we barely know.'

Claire opened her mouth, then thought better of it. The quick fluttering of butterflies of anxiety began in her chest. She made an effort to control her breathing, but felt nervousness tingling at the back of her throat and behind her ribs.

'We are leaving. Right now. And *you* are not coming with us,' Basher said, turning at last to look at Claire. His brow was heavy and he was unblinking, trembling with rage, his fist clenching and unclenching. 'When it became clear that you had, essentially, kidnapped Alex—'

'Uncle B, that's not what hap—'

'Shut up. I know you think you are an adult and that you understand everything, but you are not, and you do not.'

Basher took a deep breath in, and Claire hoped he wasn't about to say what she had dreaded he would, almost from the start. But she knew that it was coming. She felt the weight, the inevitability, and she had always known it would happen. But still, she let herself hope that he would say something else. He didn't.

'Sami called me, Claire. She told me everything. I cannot believe I ever fell for it. I always suspected that you were a grifter, obviously, but... God, you are so much fucking worse than the normal kind.' He started pacing back and forth.

Alex was looking between the two of them in confusion. 'What... what's going on, Uncle B?'

'She's a liar, Alex. She uses dead children – *children* – to make a name for herself. I should never have agreed to any of this. I should have run a mile the second you said your spirit guide was a teenage girl. Jesus!'

Claire felt a block of ice come to rest on her shoulder, as Sophie put a hand there. She stared at the floor.

'We can get through this Claire,' Sophie said, very quietly. 'We've done it before. We'll do it again.'

Basher put his hands to his head, like a goalkeeper who had just let one in during penalties at the final of the World Cup. 'Do you know, I remember it being on the news. *The Star* got a scoop on how the police were working with a medium... but I never put it together.' He resumed his slow pacing. It had to be slow: there wasn't much room for each circuit. If he paced too fast, he'd be spinning on the spot. And as he spun, he told – who? Alex? himself? her? – the story that Claire was never able, or allowed, to forget.

Just over seven years ago the police in Essex made a public appeal in a Missing Persons case. A sixteen-year-old boy had disappeared on his way home from a friend's house. He'd been drinking. He walked into a park and didn't walk out. There were no leads, and nothing was caught on CCTV. And the officer in charge got a little desperate. He was under pressure; it was a pet case for the local press. A medium answered the call. She was able to do uncanny things – such that when she said the missing boy was within sight of a castle, the police took it seriously.

'So off they went to Colchester. Oh, they must have been *so* desperate! I can sympathize, really I can.'

Claire still did not move her head to look at either of them, but she could see out of the corner of her eye that Alex was making the 'O' face that they did when they were surprised. Basher paused, as if daring her to speak, but she concentrated on the feeling of Sophie's hand instead. It was an encouragement to stay quiet; her shoulder was starting to numb, and if this dragged on much longer, it would start burning with cold.

'Of course they found nothing at Colchester. And in fact, a few days later, the boy was found. He was dead. They had lost any chance of finding him alive by going off on a wild goose chase. He'd been dumped in a pond on a golf club in Billericay. Not a castle in sight. Not for miles.'

Claire swallowed a sore feeling in her throat. She still didn't turn her head.

'And do you know what else? Do you know who the medium's so-called spirit guide actually is?'

'Sophie,' said Alex. 'She... it's Sophie. It's just Sophie. Come on, Uncle B, we know them!'

'But do you know who Sophie *is*?' Basher read off his phone: '"Sophie Watson, missing, last seen in 2007 in Oxford after a day-trip, wearing a blue tracksuit and white trainers, would be thirty-two now." That's from a bulletin from eight months ago. She's still missing. Claire was her best friend at school. Claire went to *vigils* for her. She made a big stir at the time, giving interviews to local press about how much she missed Sophie – how she hoped Sophie would come home. And when that wore off, guess who suddenly had visions of her friend? Had to be pulled out of school?' He turned on Claire. 'It is beyond belief that, even this many years later, you would still be trying to make a missing girl all about *you*. Seeking. This. Much. Attention! Sophie's parents are waiting for her to come home. The police have kept the case open. They think there's a chance Sophie is still alive somewhere! But I suppose that's not as important as you making a name for yourself, is it, Claire?'

Claire wanted to protest: *Oh yes*, she wanted to say, *I'm doing great. I'm rolling in it. Just look at this palace. Look at my glamorous lifestyle, my legions of admirers, my completely normal therapy record*. But she knew from experience that it wouldn't help. This was it; this was the other shoe dropping, like it always did eventually. Best to let it fall, and then wait for everyone to pick up their respective footwear and leave.

'So what was it?' Basher went on. 'Naked opportunism? When you happened to be close by when Nana died, you thought you would take us for all you could get? We can't trust a single thing you say! You attached yourself to us like a fucking leech. Living in my flat. Eating my ham. Convincing us that our family were killers! Well, it ends now, you fucking *parasite*.'

There was a ringing silence.

'Is that true, Claire?' asked Alex in a small voice. 'Was... Did you know Sophie? Is Sophie a missing person?'

Claire tried to speak, and failed again. So she settled for nodding. She felt a tear slide down to the end of her nose and brushed it off.

Alex stood up and walked over to stand behind Basher, facing the door. They wouldn't look at Claire, either.

'But I don't think...' they said haltingly. 'I mean, Claire isn't a bad person.'

'She is. We're going.' Basher looked back at Claire as he started to walk away, and it seemed as if he was pleading with her to say something, to refute everything, to prove him wrong.

'The castle was a poster. The boy, he was already dead when I spoke to him,' she tried, her voice cracking. 'He was being held in a house, and he looked out of a window and saw a poster on a bus stop near that golf course. It was advertising a weekend break in Colchester. It had a picture of a castle on it, so he thought he was near the castle. He got confused, that's all. He was already dead. He was confused and scared and wanted to go home. They couldn't have saved him. I tried to tell them. He was already dead.'

But she was talking to a slammed door.

Sophie removed her hand from Claire and did not put it back.

Claire had a hot shower and scrubbed the red skin of her shoulder until it was no longer cold to the touch, but she felt the shiver in her bones.

She tried to watch an old episode of *Murder Profile*, but it only made her think about what had just happened. It had happened before, when whoever she met eventually googled her name and gradually – or abruptly – ghosted her, or else confronted her, as Basher had. Yelled at her about being a sick attention-seeker. So this wasn't special. She and Sophie simply had to ride it out, like normal.

Claire often wondered how people felt after shouting at her. Was it cathartic?

Sophie hovered around, looking blank and stroppy. 'Can we watch something else?' she asked.

'No. I want to watch this,' lied Claire.

'You've seen it before.'

'So?'

'Ohmigod. Don't be a child, C.'

'I'm not a fucking child. And don't call me "C" – since when do you call me "C"?' snapped Claire. 'You're never going to be as interesting as Alex, you know that?'

Soph flinched. 'Yeah, duh. I'll never get the chance. So what's your excuse?'

Claire ignored her, but Sophie walked around to stand in front of the TV.

'No, I'm serious, Claire. What *is* your excuse? You're alive, you have a life to do things with, and you... you don't do *anything* except watch this stupid fucking show over and over again. And drive people away. I'd have fucked off by now, if I could.'

Claire was genuinely open-mouthed. 'Are you serious? What's my excuse?' She felt her voice rising. 'You! You are – you stupid... fucking... *cow*. My entire existence is about you. I can't have anything else, because you're always, always here!'

'Like you could survive without me – like you could do anything without me. You need me. You wouldn't even have a job without me.'

'I only need you because you exist, idiot!' Claire was full-on yelling now, tears that she wasn't even aware of streaming down her face. 'I could have a normal job if it wasn't for you, I could have friends. I wouldn't have had four years of pointless fucking therapy.'

'We *had* friends, stupid. Basher and Alex knew about me and they liked me. I'm so fucking sick of *you*.'

'Yeah? Join the club. It's not like they left because of me. They left because of you – you're the package deal that nobody wants to buy, dickhead. You're the one that fucked up, talking to that missing kid. There wouldn't even *be* anything to look up about me, otherwise! How are you not getting this?'

Claire became aware that she was standing and they were both shouting at each other; the thought floated through her brain, mostly unobserved, that she hoped her neighbours assumed she was on the phone. Her face and neck were hot and wet, from the rage and shame and tears and guilt.

Sophie couldn't cry. Her eyes were like bowls of water that you could drop copper pennies in: the water seemed to swell and swell, but no matter how many coins you threw in, the surface tension wouldn't break, it would

293

never overflow. But the air was horribly chill. The condensation on the windows was sparkling, little white ferns were tracing their way across the corners of the TV screen, and even the ceiling leak had stopped, becoming a tiny, grimy icicle that gave the impression time had stood still. Claire did not pause to take a breath.

'I have to be responsible for your fuck-ups, but you don't have to be responsible for anything. You have genuinely ruined my life.' The totality of the silence that followed this was so frightening that Claire felt like she had ripped a black hole in the world and was about to disappear into it.

Then Sophie broke it, and her voice was more than speech, it was an expression of force. It was like the terrible, sunken toll of the church bell in a flooded town. Claire felt it reverberate in her chest as if it were empty, as if she herself were hollow.

'It's not my fucking fault I'm dead!' Sophie screamed.

And because all Claire had left was the truth: *'It's not mine, either. But maybe you fucking deserve it!'*

PART III

I have been bent and broken, but – I hope – into a better shape.

Charles Dickens, *Great Expectations*

15

Cold Comfort

It was Monday morning again. Claire was lying in bed in the foetal position. Her toes and knees were braced against the wall, so she couldn't move. Her phone was playing through back-episodes of a podcast in which three loud Americans made fun of conspiracy theories, but she wasn't listening to it.

She and Soph were still not speaking to each other. Claire was starting to wonder if she would eventually lose the ability to speak. If she thought about it too hard, she couldn't remember what her voice sounded like. Sometimes she would whisper something to herself to check. 'Hello. Hello, Claire. Hello, hello, stop, go, goodbye.'

She felt hollow. Hollow and brittle. Like a chocolate rabbit. Absurd.

She lay with Sophie's butterfly hair-claw held loosely in her fist. Sometimes she woke up and it was gone, and she scrabbled around until she found it tangled somewhere in the sheets. It looked like the metal spring was coming loose on one side.

Sometimes she felt like she was chained to the bottom of a vast sea, and a storm was raging above the surface and she was being pushed by great swells that she could not see: it would relent for a moment, or even for hours, and then another huge invisible wave would overcome her and push her, and strain her limbs against restraints that would not snap. It hurt so terribly, but all she could do was cry out into her pillow. Each time she felt she could not bear it, but, alas, it seemed she had no choice.

Sometimes she felt the air grow cold and she knew that Soph was looking at her. Claire woke up in the night and Sophie was there, watching. Other times, Sophie went out to stand on the street, as if trying to get as far away from Claire as possible.

In between lying in bed, Claire had mostly been watching *Murder Profile* and listening to podcasts. She was eating a lot of sliced bread, straight from the bag. Her mouth was getting very yeasty. And she was running out of bread.

That afternoon she reached into the bag and found it was empty. And for some reason it was this, more than anything else, that motivated her to get up and make motions towards re-joining her life. She needed bread. She would have to go out to buy more bread.

Claire did this, and noted that buying bread had made her go overdrawn again. She had transferred the money that Hugh had sent her into a savings account, ring-fenced away from the rest of her life. Blood-money that she felt weird about touching.

The shop assistant's haunted expression was enough to make Claire think she needed to get out and talk to more people. Her regular customers were safe – people who wouldn't shout at her. And they would give her money. A two-birds sort of situation.

Her life seemed like a sort of slow-moving train that she had hopped off and now merely needed to jog a bit, in order to hop back on. It was a bit of effort, but fundamentally not much had changed. This, too, was somewhat depressing. Even her own life could function pretty well without her.

She had postponed or cancelled her regulars while she was investigating The Case, so she decided to call Donna, who always cheered her up and had a need for her services.

Donna was a woman in her seventies who combined pragmatism with a streak of delightful hedonism; as long as she wasn't hurting anyone else, she did whatever she felt would make her happy – and this included hiring a medium every few months to bicker with her dead older sister, Michelle, about TV soaps. They were both still hanging around in the two-up, two-down house that had belonged to their parents before them and Claire liked going to see them, especially because Donna always provided a hearty, but slightly grim old-person meal, like faggots in gravy, followed by prunes in custard. Technically, she did shout at Claire. But not in that way.

'HELLO!' said the profoundly deaf Donna, as she answered the phone. It was a crackly old house phone and Donna frequently blew out the line with her volume. Claire usually found her own volume rising, in sympathy.

'Hello. Donna! It's Claire!'

'OOOOH, CLAIRE...'

After two minutes' worth of small talk that took about ten minutes of mutual loud talking, and then a much more confusing conversation while they found a date and time that suited Donna (who had to look up her engagements in an honest-to-goodness paper diary), they were able to pin down a time for a seance the following week. Sophie's involvement would have to be a cross-that-bridge situation. Claire scribbled down the appointment on the first thing she found in her pocket, which happened to be the ticket from Brighton to London.

'WE'LL HAVE LIVER AND ONIONS!' said Donna in delight. 'THE BUTCHER SAYS HE'S GOING TO KEEP A NICE BIT OF BACON FOR ME!'

'What was that – sorry?'

'BACK BACON! WHO'S YOUR BUTCHER? YOU SHOULD TAKE MEAT CUTS SERIOUSLY. BACON!'

Claire froze. She suddenly had a strange feeling, like a bubble was floating down from the ceiling somewhere and she had to catch it, before it hit the table and exploded in very small violence. But if she moved too fast, it would also pop into nothing.

'Thank you, Donna. I'll have to call you back,' she said, suddenly almost whispering. She hung up. Possibly Donna would be completely unaware that she had done so and would continue shouting about bacon for several minutes.

What had she been doing? She had been looking at the train ticket, and Donna had been talking about lunch. Claire looked at the ticket again. It had several things scrawled on it: a swirly doodle, half a phone number, the name 'Arrowhead Beacon', Donna's appointment.

There it was again. Her mind snagged. Something about what Donna had said, and the name Arrowhead Beacon, was making her brain sluggishly try to fire off something – it was just very bad at it. This was the bit Sophie was good at: the logical connections. Claire did the emotion and the flights of fancy. She felt like a cat trying to walk in socks.

She tried out combinations, like rotating jigsaw pieces side-by-side.

Who's your butcher? Arrowhead Beacon.

Arrowhead Beacon. Meat cuts seriously.

Back bacon. Arrowhead Beacon.

Arrowhead bacon.

Arrowhead bacon? Bacon seriously.

Seriously bacon.

Beacon. Bacon.

'Oh my God. Oh my God!' Claire yelled out loud, jumping to her feet. '"I'm serious about *Beacon*!" Ohmigod, Soph – oh.'

Sophie wasn't there.

Claire dropped her triumphantly raised arms back down to her sides. Shit! Shitshitshit. Right. She decided to have a shower first, because the smell of her own hair was quite distracting and it was at least a *decision* that she could make *decisively*.

Then she got a pen and made a list of the top twenty accounting firms in the City. She made this list very neatly on the first page of a fresh notebook that she found under the Ikea table. Claire then spent an hour and a half ringing each of them, asking if they had any employees called Michael who matched Michael's brief description, and if he could please call her back, if so.

Then she remembered the printout she had nicked from the things Michael had left in Monty's office. Hope blazed strong in her chest that it would be a smoking gun – an email from Hugh to Monty saying, 'What should we do about that person we murdered and buried on our property?' perhaps.

Claire was quite disappointed that it turned out to be an apparently insignificant email from Michael to Monty, sent in July last year:

Hi Monty,

Just wanted to flag up some irregularities I've noticed in one of the shell accounts. I'm sure it's nothing, but it would be good to check some of the transactions going to one of the shells – Arrowhead Beacon. It's my job to be thorough, after all!

Thanks,

Michael

It was disappointingly boring.

No, that was the wrong way to think about it. Though Claire was loath to admit it, she needed to think about it like she would if Sophie was here to talk it through with her. So…

'Okay. Michael kept it – the email was important enough that he wanted to have a copy of it. Why a physical copy, though? Maybe because…' And here Claire resisted theorizing that Michael was going to pass it to a secret third party, or that it was part of a larger cache of documents that he had been smuggling, one page per day, out of the office. She forced her mind onto a less made-for-TV track. 'Because he wanted to show it to someone, but Monty's company can check the emails that their employees send.'

Talking out loud seemed to be helping. That, at least, was accurate from TV.

'So he couldn't forward it outside without the company maybe seeing. So he printed it off. And… and it was in the back of a notepad because he didn't want anyone else to see it accidentally. So that means… Hmm. I suppose it means Michael printed it off just before he left the company, when he knew something really was up, as double proof that he wasn't in on it. But then he probably forgot about it.'

Although it would be good if he'd written a message on it in lemon juice or some other invisible ink, she added internally. You check that with heat, don't you? Her oven had gas hobs, and she wasn't sure that would work.

Claire put a pin in that idea and started ringing the accounting firms on the list from the top down again, this time asking for Michael Brewin, because the email had revealed his last name.

Firm twelve recognized the name and promised to pass the message on. In a flash of inspiration, Claire added that it was 'about Beacon', reckoning that it was likely to get a faster response.

She was right. Michael called back to ask what she wanted, and when Claire said she needed to talk about the Wellington-Forge family and their accounts, Michael gave an extremely deep, long sigh.

'Okay. I'm sick to death of the lot of them. I'll tell you everything, as long as nobody ever mentions that family to me again. What do you want to know?'

This was easier than Claire had expected. 'Not over the phone,' she said. 'Someone could be listening.'

'What? Who?'

'I dunno – whoever. It's sensitive information.'

'This is... All right, fine, but after today I am never thinking or speaking about Monty and his dad ever again.'

They agreed to meet, after Michael had finished work, for coffee in Battersea. Which Claire supposed counted as neutral ground for both of them.

As the time got closer to the moment when she had to leave, Claire began to worry. There was still no sign of Sophie. She hadn't been anywhere without Sophie for most of her life. But she didn't technically have to wait for her... Claire paced around like a nervous dog for a bit, then put on a scarf, a long-sleeved top, a hoodie and a jacket. She zipped everything up and pulled up her hood before she left.

After she'd been walking for a few minutes she felt the little pull that meant Sophie was being tugged after her. It didn't happen often, because they were rarely apart, but whenever the connection was tested there was a sensation. Not unpleasant, merely an awareness. Almost as if Claire could feel the bump of an ingrown hair, but in her whole body. By the time she entered the Tube she could tell, without looking, that Sophie was closer behind her. *It Follows*, but with a noughties teenager in a shitty mood.

By the time they got to Battersea it was clear that Sophie was curious, but still too proud to get involved. As Claire went into a small local café, Sophie followed and stayed in one corner, just on the edge of earshot. Claire kept her hood up, so that she wouldn't have to look at her out of the corner of her eye. A bargain-bucket Banquo.

Michael came in a few minutes later. He was as obtrusively handsome and tall as the others had said, but he was also, Claire noticed, slightly hunched over and stooping, as if trying to make himself look smaller. He came over to Claire – one of the only other people in there, and definitely the only one wearing a hood up and ugly shades indoors – and asked very politely if she was waiting for him.

He sat down and they looked at each other. Inevitably Claire blinked first, but she still wanted to be cool, professional and mysterious, so she got out the email and slid it across the table towards him. Michael's face was expressionless, but in the way it is when a face is trying really hard not to have any expression.

'How did you get this?' he asked, taking it. Claire noticed how clean and neat his nails were. Michael frowned. 'And why is it a bit burnt?'

'How I got it isn't important,' said Claire seriously. 'It was burnt in the course of... er, classified investigations.'

The interview technique of being outwardly inept seemed to relax Michael. 'Okay then, we'll ignore that for now,' he said. 'Who are you? You're clearly not in finance, and obviously not police.'

'Yeah, *all right*. Jesus!' Claire decided to drop the terrible, short-lived act. 'I'm sort of a family friend of the Wellington-Forges. Well, I'm a friend of some of the family. Actually, maybe none of them.'

'So you're... a family enemy?' Michael looked confused, but also like he was trying not to laugh at her.

'I went to university with Figgy.'

'The waspy daughter?'

'Yeah. Anyway, not this weekend just gone, but the one before I was invited to The Cloisters...'

Claire told him the truncated version of the story that she was now used to giving, without the ghosts and, in this case, replacing 'There was an 'orrible murder' with a vague impartation that some illegal shit was possibly going down.

'And I don't really care about this Arrowhead Beacon thing, but I think it has something to do with that. Because Basher heard you arguing and he thought you were talking about breakfast, but you weren't, were you? You were saying you were serious about Beacon.'

'Well spotted. I'd have said you're probably right about Beacon being the cause, except that it turns out it doesn't really matter.'

Michael sighed heavily again, as if steeling himself to continue.

'Arrowhead Beacon is a pretty standard shell company attached to Monty's firm. Most places have more than one; it's maybe a bit weird for a legal firm, but they're corporate lawyers. Good for moving money around, I suppose. I was seconded to PP&R – sorry, Parker, Parker and Renwick – to do a general wash and brush-up of their accounts, make sure they won't get stung with a whopping tax bill, check that nobody had stolen anything from the pension pot. That sort of thing.'

'An MOT, but for office finances?'

'Exactly. But a few months in, I find Beacon. And it's... fishy. Being a conscientious accountant, I sent Monty that email straight away because, as a conscientious manager, he'd want to know. Except that he gets cross and starts putting pressure on me *not* to look into it. Which makes me want to keep looking into it. Eventually Monty invites me to his family home to work through a heap of files and receipts. That's unusual, obviously, but I decided to go, because by this stage I'm pretty convinced that the family business is something to do with it.'

Claire was genuinely on the edge of her seat. 'Go on,' she prompted. Sophie had edged closer, with practised nonchalance.

'I managed to sneak some time in their office, with help from their estate manager lady – Maude or Mary, or something – and even just a quick glance through their paper files confirmed it. Monty is skimming... embezzling, basically, and using The Cloisters to do so.'

'*WHOA!*' said Claire.

'Yes, that's what I thought,' said Michael drily. 'They've not been that clever about it really. PP&R books a couple of legitimate events at The Cloisters every year, so if you're skimming the account and see the transactions coming up, there's cover for it. But there are way more transactions than are reasonably legitimate, so if you look into it in any depth whatsoever, it becomes very obvious. Plus, it's only one step removed. Monty is not the Machiavelli of financial crime.'

'Yeah, his dad paid me directly from that account actually,' said Claire. Michael snorted at this.

'I think it's probably a family slush fund at this point,' he said. 'The Cloisters looked like it was running at a hefty loss, otherwise. Anyway after the weekend I was down there, I decided to back off, but to keep having a look discreetly, work the rest of my time at PP&R and then report everything to my boss at my firm, when I was out. I'd already got in touch with HMRC.' He sighed again. 'Except it doesn't matter. My boss told me to leave it, and HMRC never did a full investigation themselves.'

'What, really?' Claire was incredulous.

'Apparently, as crimes go, it's not really important or sexy enough. No money-laundering for the Mob, no millions in import and export scamming, just regular greed. It was implied to me that most executives every-where are feathering their own nests, and if we report one of them, we have to report all of them – and then we wouldn't have any clients, and London wouldn't have any corporate offices. So there you go. Whole lot of stress and bother for nothing.'

'Hmm.'

Claire took a big sip of her tea, as cover to think. She had not expected this to be such a dead end.

'Did you see anything weird at all that weekend?' she asked, feeling a bit deflated. But in for a penny.

'Well, I didn't know there was going to be a police officer there. That scared me a bit. I avoided her the whole time.'

This seemed fair.

Michael paused. 'Also, the family themselves are awful,' he said, having decided that a family enemy was safe enough for this. 'The mum kept saying, "Oh, good for *you!*" to me, about any personal or professional achieve-ments that I mentioned.'

'Oh, actually,' Claire said, suddenly remembering another important issue, 'where did you go? You said you were going to make a call, but you never came back and the timings don't match up.'

'Yes, I am afraid I did what we City professionals call "a lie",' said Michael. 'I asked that other man – the boyfriend, Kevin – to drop me at the station instead and not tell anyone; and to tell them that he drove me to make a phone call. So that I could leave. I trusted that everyone would be too self-involved to really notice or care.'

Claire leaned her face in one hand and drummed her fingers with the other. That did make sense: Kevin got back sooner, because he hadn't actually driven as far as they'd thought. This, too, was disappointingly mundane.

'In fact,' said Michael, after draining the last of his coffee, 'I was a bit indiscreet with him. I say "indiscreet". I was angry and told him almost everything during the car ride. I felt like I had to give him a reason to cover for me, I suppose. I was asking him to lie to his girlfriend and her family, after all. Kevin got really annoyed about the whole thing, though. More annoyed than I was. Started slapping the steering wheel and going on about the bourgeoisie and hypocrisy, and how borders are just lines in the sand. Called me "brother".'

'Hmm,' said Claire again, still tapping her fingers and almost forgetting Michael was there.

'So I'm going to go now,' he said eventually. 'And I'm going to take this,' he said, wafting the printed email.

'Huh? Oh. Er... yes, fine. Thank you,' replied Claire, her mind elsewhere. 'Glad you're not dead.'

'Sorry?'

'Oh, nothing,' she said.

She waited until the bell over the door clanged as he left, then turned to look at Sophie. She was standing a lot closer, but she still glanced away when their eyes met, like a drunk man on a train pretending he wasn't looking the whole time. Claire's heart sank a little more into the hollow in her chest. She thought she'd at least earned a bit of acknowledgement for a successful lone interview, and for some bloody good detecting.

After some hesitation, Claire sent Alex a text explaining that she had met Michael, and maybe there was more to Kevin than they'd thought, but that Mattie was still the number-one vic option. And that she was sorry and missed them, and hoped they were okay. Pressing Send made her sunken heart thud.

When they got home, she had a voicemail. Alex had tried to call while she was on the Tube. 'Hello, C. And S? Maybe? I dunno. I dunno why I'm calling really. Except to say maybe you should let it go? It's Nana's funeral on Thursday. Just feels like a place to end. You shouldn't come. Sorry.' They did actually sound apologetic. 'Okay. Bye.'

Claire spent the rest of the afternoon lying in bed crying, either big racking sobs that seemed to come from nowhere or the baby-sniffles of a sad, unhugged puppy. By the time the sun had set she'd exhausted herself, but lay there in the dark, unable to sleep.

After a while – Claire didn't know how long – Sophie came in and sat on the bed.

'That was good, working out the Beacon thing. I'm impressed.'

'Thanks. Hey, why were you so sure it wasn't Michael who had died?'

'The skeleton had long hair. Michael's bald.'

'Oh. You're right; it was stupid that none of the rest of us noticed that.'

'Yeah. I was being petty, though.'

'Yeah.'

They stayed there in silence for another while.

'Can't sleep?' said Sophie.

'Naw.'

Sophie lay down next to her. 'I'm sorry,' she said.

'Me too.'

After a few moments, Soph took Claire's hand. She actually held it, like it was a seance. They used to do this when Claire was younger and couldn't sleep, before exams or after a bad date, or because of the relentless prodding and poking and questions about why she thought she could talk to her dead friend.

Claire felt the battery *zip* and didn't fight it. After a couple of minutes she was very cold and very sleepy, and then after a few seconds more she was very warm and fuzzy, even though she could tell the sheets and the room, and her skin, were all the same smooth coldness as one carved block of marble.

Her eyelids drooped and Claire wondered, as they finally closed, if this was what it was like to freeze to death. It wouldn't be so bad, she thought.

16

Family Values

That Wednesday, Claire and Sophie were on a bus. Claire loved public transport, but did not like buses. Trains had to stick to where they were going, whereas buses could decide to pull wild-card moves, and frequently did. Also, people on buses seemed to be much more given to getting up and gobbing on the floor, or doing weird shit like shredding an umbrella to pieces or sicking up in coffee cups. When you got on a bus there was a 50 per cent chance you were stepping into a holding cell for the damned. That didn't seem entirely inappropriate for her and Sophie. But luckily they were the only people on the bus. It was that sort of route, winding through scrubby grass fields and bare hedgerows that seemed, to Claire, to be indistinguishable from each other, or from the hedgerows of any country lane she had ever seen. They could have been on the roads to The Cloisters, except that they were quite a long way from there.

They had come on a strange sort of Hail Mary mission. Even though Alex had advised them to drop it, Claire and Sophie had spent most of Tuesday talking about it and decided that neither of them wanted to yet. It would be like leaving an unsolved jigsaw all over your coffee table, even though you'd just started to fit the weird-shaped pieces together. Sophie had also said that maybe, if they could figure out what had really happened, it would be a reason to talk to Alex and Basher and they could maybe, possibly, be friends again. If Claire examined this idea for too long, it became the vain hope of some desperate, lonely children, so she kept it in her peripheral vision, where it was the noble hope of brave heroes. Because the other thing was that Claire kept remembering the agony of that ghost in the library. Their unending pain. And she and Soph had agreed that it would be good to help them, if possible.

Also, she kept remembering times when Basher had given her an awkward side hug or when their knees had touched on the sofa, and the feel of the skinny heat of his body under his hoodie. It was nice to believe that he might think well of her again. Sometimes she would type out a message to him on her phone and imagine that he had their conversation open as well and could see the 'CLAIRE IS TYPING' ellipsis. But she never sent anything.

The problem was that they were running out of trails to follow. Michael was clearly alive, so he could be crossed off the list as 'not dead' for absolute definite (although a radical defence lawyer might argue that Claire speaking to someone wasn't cast-iron proof in her specific case, obviously). Mattie was less of a sure thing: she'd been betraying the family to the Du Lotte Hotels chain, so Clem and Hugh had a motive to bump her off, plus her husband was being paid off for doing something, and her son was upset at the family. But while Claire had no definitive proof that she was alive, there wasn't really any evidence she was dead, either, so Mattie was a bit of a dead end, without help from Alex and Basher.

But there was one thin, tenuous lead that hadn't been explored and that Claire could follow by herself: Kevin's parents.

After a lot of back and forth, Sophie had agreed that the logical thing to do was to verify that Kevin was definitely, 100 per cent alive, because when they thought about it, they realized they hadn't spoken to him in person, either. And if he was alive, then they could try and definitively find Mattie and then, if necessary, widen the pool of potential victims and go back to the drawing board. Usually one's parents will know whether or not you're alive. Not in every case, obviously, but it would be insensitive to mention that to Sophie.

Back at The Cloisters, in what now seemed about a decade ago rather just over a week, Figgy had mentioned that Kevin's parents were 'Sue and Jeremy, lovely little cottage in South Withemswall'. So now, in a reckless move, they were on the way to find Sue and Jeremy and their lovely little cottage in South Withemswall. Since these were the only directions they had, they were just... on a bus to South Withemswall.

After almost an hour they arrived at their stop. Claire checked the time. It was already nearly 4 p.m. She didn't want to get back home at 2 a.m., but she was now concerned that she wouldn't be able to get back home at all. She hadn't packed any clothes, simply grabbed her backpack and headed out, and she also hadn't checked if there was anywhere to stay in South Withemswall. But she wasn't voicing these concerns to Sophie. She felt that her successful locating and interrogation of Michael had set a precedent of competence.

South Withemswall was halfway between a town and a village. The houses had red-tiled roofs and visible beams. In the summer there would probably be rambling dog roses and apple trees full of ripening green fruit. The bus stop was next to a red phone box that didn't seem to have been used as a toilet. She could see a village shop, and a pub further down the road. It looked like there was even a school as well. There was bunting.

'This,' observed Sophie, 'is bucolic as *fuck*.'

Claire's vague plan had been to ask people where Sue and Jeremy lived, but because it was cold and damp here too, there was a dearth of people visiting each other with baskets of preserves, or helpful kids playing with skipping ropes. Sophie meandered down the road, scuffing her heels as she went.

'Where are you going?' asked Claire.

In answer, Sophie pointed: rising above the big green cloud of a yew tree was a squat church spire. Claire dropped her head and groaned like a teenager. *Gaaauuuuuuuud! UGH!*

She wasn't in the mood for the particularly self-involved, depressive brand of spook that hung around graveyards and churches. It wasn't their fault, really. If she had to spend eternity arguing with other dead people over what was basically a parking space, and listening to 'All Things Bright and Beautiful' every weekend, she'd probably not be a laugh a minute, either.

On the other hand, graveyard ghosts tended to be less starved for attention, since they had more people to talk to. And Sophie's logic, as far as she could guess it, was sound: they needed to ask locals for directions, and there was nobody more local than an elderly churchyard ghost.

Withemswall church's permanent congregation was a Just William-esque schoolboy cheerfully wellying a ghostly football around the yard; an old woman in black Edwardian dress and veil, who was watching him with grandmotherly affection; a man with a big moustache and sideburns, wearing a suit with very flared trousers (who was sitting against his own headstone in a carefully despondent manner); and a younger woman in a black poodle-skirted dress, who was looking at him with undisguised disdain. She was holding a lit cigarette that curled smoke into the air, but never burned down. Claire lit a cigarette of her own and let Sophie go ahead of her. It usually went better that way.

'Hello,' she said. 'I'm Sophie. This is my friend Claire. What's going on?'

The man seemed quite surprised, but recovered quickly and went back to looking tortured and interesting. 'Oh, what a question!' he lamented. 'What a world! Nothing's going on, and everything.'

The girl rolled her eyes. 'First new people he's been able to speak to in ages. Howard, baby, I'm pretty sure the sad poet act won't work on them.' She took a deep drag on the cigarette and muttered, *sotto voce*, 'Especially if you recite any of your poems.'

The older woman, who was keeping count of successful keepy-ups for the boy, chimed in to say that they were both being very rude. 'I'm Miss Pinkett, this boisterous young man is Luke, and that's Maisie and Howard,' she said.

Maisie pointed to each of them in turn: 'Old age, flu, coughing up a lung, writing poetry so terrible that he died to spare the world.'

'Drowning,' corrected Howard.

'Sorry, drowning.'

'I always get those two mixed up as well,' said Claire.

Maisie laughed and clapped her hands together. 'Oh, you are just a gas!' she said. 'What brings you here anyway?'

'We're looking for a couple called Sue and Jeremy, who live in a cottage somewhere around here,' said Sophie.

'Now there's a coincidence,' said Miss Pinkett. Claire was immediately suspicious. She didn't think there were such things as coincidences in murder investigations,

318

because Smitty on *Murder Profile* said as much at least every other episode.

'Now, Luke – now, calm down and come here to talk to these nice ladies. They're looking for your old house. Jeremy is Luke's grand-nephew – isn't he, Luke?'

Luke stopped kicking the football and stood fidgeting in front of them. He had ruddy cheeks and radiated big-paper-bag-full-of-aniseed-balls energy.

'So what if he is?' he said, with the attitude of someone who treated all new grown-ups as if they were his head-master. 'Those lot are boring. They used to come and visit me and my brother's graves, but now they barely ever do.'

'Is your brother around?' asked Soph.

'No. I'm glad, though; he was about a thousand years old when he died. He wasn't fun any more, either. Old people aren't fun. Well,' he added kindly, 'apart from ol' Pinko. You're all right, aren't you, Miss Pinkett?'

'Have you ever met your great-grand-nephew, Luke? His name's Kevin,' asked Claire.

'Dunno if that's what his name is, but he came here once, ages ago, and ol' Rogers, the vicar, got cross and chucked him out for talking about pagan religions and saying God wasn't a proper God, or something.'

'Well, that definitely sounds like Kevin,' said Claire. 'Can you give us directions to your old house, please, Luke?'

He did, very importantly. It turned out to only be about five minutes' walk away. 'Why d'you want to see them anyway?' Luke asked. He was starting to lose inter-est, though, and was fiddling with his football.

'Your great-grand-nephew is a friend of mine and I wanted to stop in and say hello to his parents while we were here,' said Claire, who was impressed by how good she was getting at lying on the spot.

'Huh. All right then.' Luke paused. 'Can you go and check on what they've done to my room, and come back and say?'

'I'll try,' said Claire. 'But we should probably be off now. It's nearly teatime already.'

'I miss having tea. All right. Bye!' He ran off and booted his football at a statue of a cherub.

'So, Sophie,' said Maisie. 'What was it that got you?'

Sophie looked straight at her. 'I don't know,' she said. The ghosts shared a moment of understanding and made sympathetic noises. 'It's all right. It doesn't seem to matter that much any more.'

'Tragedy, death, dinner – so many rich primal urges, now sloughing off us like so much... like... like gravy off a duck's back,' said Howard, his voice as thick with melancholy as, presumably, the gravy.

'Oh, do shut the fuck up, Howard dear,' said Miss Pinkett.

Claire and Sophie left as Maisie's roaring laughter filled the churchyard.

'It occurs to me,' mused Sophie, 'that we have not taken much advantage of our special talents during this investigation. Like – ohmigod, babes. I can walk through walls. We can talk to dead people. We should have been doing that the whole time.'

It took a little longer than expected to find Sue and Jeremy's cottage because it was getting dark, and because South Withemswall had changed a little in the last hundred years, so Luke's directions were not quite accurate. After a bit of backtracking, they ended up at a likely cottage and knocked at the door, and were then directed by Sue and Jeremy's neighbour to the house opposite.

Kevin's parents' house was a whitewashed thatched cottage that was long and squat, with little windows deep in the straw eaves. There was a horseshoe on the door. Claire was about to knock when Sophie declared, 'Go hard or go home!' and strode straight through it.

Claire loitered on the doorstep, unsure what to do, until she heard a muffled yell from Sophie.

'They're in. They're watching a recording of *The Chase*. I'm going to look around.'

Claire raised her hand to knock, momentarily panicked about knocking in a weird or suspicious way, and in a spasm of terror ended up doing 'Shave and a Haircut'. Soph's head and shoulders appeared from an upstairs window. 'LOL. Although I bet loads of people do that around here.'

Eventually the door was opened by a short woman with very freckly skin and wispy hair that looked as if it had once been chestnut-coloured. She was wearing a calf-length denim skirt, fluffy slippers and a big cable-knit jumper. A blast of heat and savoury cooking smells came with her. She smiled and waited.

'Yes, hello?' she said eventually.

'Oh, right. Er, sorry. Is it, um – it's Sue, right? My name's Claire, I'm a friend of Kevin's. We met whilst travelling in, er, India.'

'Gosh, I didn't think he'd been there.'

'Europe. Probably Europe actually. I've just been around so much that I get mixed up. But Kevin always said how nice this part of the world was for, er, things, and I thought I would drop in and say hello while I was passing through. I hope that's all right.'

'Oh, right! Well, yes. Do come in for a cup of tea, I suppose. Yes, that's lovely.' Sue seemed even more unsure than Claire was, but in the battle between ingrained politeness and feeling uncomfortable with strangers, politeness won. In fairness, it had awkwardness on its side, to deliver a flanking attack.

Claire was briskly introduced to Jeremy, who was wearing a similar jumper but in a different colour (Claire was later told that they were hand-made by Sue). He seemed mostly to want to be left alone to finish watching *The Chase*, so Sue took her into a slate-flagged kitchen to make her a cup of tea. The mug said 'PUG OF TEA' and had a pug on it. Claire took it in red fingers and noticed, as she often did, that she had grown very cold without realizing it. Sue noticed too and asked Claire if she wanted hand-warmers. It was the most mothered Claire had felt for years. No wonder the Wellington-Forges had been so upsetting for Kevin.

He was an only child, it seemed. There were pictures of him everywhere: bouncing baby, chubby toddler, crusty student, crustier adult.

'So you met him while he was Interrailing?' Sue asked.

'Yeah,' said Claire. 'It was... wow, can't even remember when now. Ha-ha! Just such a... er, wild time, you know, everyone gets thrown in together. Kevin was so, um, passionate. And knowledgeable. He had so many interesting thoughts about things.'

Sue nodded and smiled; Claire's furious inventing obviously sounded true to life.

'We've fallen out of touch recently, though,' she added.

Sue rolled her eyes. 'You and me both! Goodness, yes. Kevin texts us every so often from South America, but we haven't seen him for a whole year. Imagine! And coming up on Christmas again.' She lowered her voice. 'I think he's having a bit of a – whatdyoucallit? Like the Mormons.'

'Rumspringa,' said Sophie, walking in.

'Rumspringa!' said Sue, finding the word. 'A late one. He had a bad break-up, you see, and he sent a text to say he was going back to South America, because he'd found himself there before and wanted to do it again. I do miss him, though! And Jeremy misses him too, of course,' she added, clearly being the person who had to write all the birthday cards.

She topped up their mugs of tea again, just as a kitchen timer in the shape of a red pepper buzzed on the side.

Sue cried, 'The casserole!' and pulled a big orange dish out of the oven. It was pheasant in rich brown gravy, with carrots and potatoes and celery and thick suet dumplings. Claire had a brief flashback to the Red Line, and to the soft, beautiful birds hanging by the back door at The Cloisters.

'You... you should stay for dinner!' Sue said, after only a moment's hesitation. 'I'd love to hear stories about your travels and adventures.'

'This should be good,' said Sophie. 'Actually, no, it'll be fine. Sorry. You'll be fine. I can help – I've been in Kevin's room and looked around. Relax.'

'Thank you,' said Claire, looking at nobody in particular. 'That's nice of you.'

In fact dinner *was* mostly fine. Jeremy bore with stoicism the surprise appearance of a stranger. The only wobble came when he asked what brought her to the area, and Claire – a woman wearing a thin wool coat, unlined hoodie and canvas trainers, and carrying only a small fashion-brand rucksack – said 'hiking'. Jeremy raised his eyebrows, but said nothing. Sue sometimes tried to winkle out an anecdote about her son, but with Sophie's help, Claire was able to fob her off, or say something about *Chicken Soup for the Soul* (which, it transpired, Kevin had bought for his mum as well).

When her dish was clean, Claire excused herself to go to the toilet and, on the way back, Sophie directed her to Kevin's room.

'I think this was probably Luke's as well,' she said. 'But it has a big Kev vibe now.'

It was quite small, with white walls and black exposed beams like the rest of the house, and it was neat – but neat in a way that suggested Sue had tidied up a bit, not that Kevin kept it neat. There were a lot of books about meditation written by singers from punk bands, and some glow-in-the-dark stars stuck on the wall by the head of the bed. They'd clearly been stuck up by seven-year-old Kevin and left up by adult Kevin, and Claire suddenly felt a lump form in her throat. Kevin was a bit of a little boy, really.

There was a knot of necklaces and bracelets hanging off one of the bedposts. A lot of them featured the same design of a bright blue eye shape on a royal-blue background. Claire was sure she'd seen it somewhere.

'That's the *evil eye*,' said Sophie mysteriously. 'He must collect them or something.'

'Do you know that because the dead have a connection to all – you know – mystical symbols or whatever?'

'No, I know that because all the tourist shops were selling them that time we went on a school trip to Greece. *Ohmigod,* do you ever pay attention to anyfuckingthing?'

One wall had a cork board covered in printed-out photos, each carefully labelled in the margin. Kevin was in all of them – raising glasses in blurry focus with a whole group in a French bar, with his arm around a couple in a hostel in Vietnam, riding bikes in front of Swiss mountains – and always with people. Never alone, never only him in front of a landmark. There were lots in airports and train stations, too. Claire stretched out a finger towards one.

'Sue's behind you,' said Sophie.

It was very useful to have a talking alarm system. Claire made sure she didn't pause, and touched the photo like she would have if there was nobody else there. It was a selfie, of Kevin with another man about the same age, sitting on a plane. It looked like they'd just taken their seats, because Kevin was still holding his boarding pass. He looked happy.

'You can have it, if you like,' said Sue. 'I'm sure he wouldn't mind. He loved taking photos with people.'

Claire hoped Sue didn't notice that she herself featured in none of them. 'Oh I wouldn't... I can't...'

'It's all right, Claire. I can tell from how you talk about him... You miss him too, don't you?'

'Oh-ho!' yelled Sophie. 'Ohmigod, plot twist! She thinks you had the hots for Kevin.'

Claire curled her toes in her shoes. 'Yes,' she said, looking at this very kind middle-aged lady who had given her dinner. 'I, uh, I'm afraid I do... carry a torch for Kevin.'

'Don't be embarrassed,' said Sue.

Claire realized she was blushing.

'You know, I did think it was funny, you calling him Kevin.'

'What do you mean?' Claire asked.

'Well, it's not his name of course.'

'It... it isn't?' Claire went from blushing to blanched. It was possible that any semblance of cover was about to be blown. 'I'm sorry, I only ever knew him as Kevin.'

'No-o-o, he's not Kevin really. He's Jeremy too, after his dad, but we all called him Jerry. I don't know where "Kevin" came from. I thought he'd only really been called that the past couple of years by his girlfriend – well, his ex, don't worry – and that set of London friends.'

'Oh. I don't know what to say – he's always been Kevin to me,' said Claire, stammering a bit. She was shocked.

'Goodness me, don't give it a second thought. But you go ahead and take that photo. I expect you'll want to be off soon. Not hanging around with a pair of boring old fuddy-duddies like me and Jeremy!'

'Yes, of course, you're right – I mean, no, you're not fuddy-duddies at all. Thank you so much for dinner.'

Claire smiled brightly as she bid Sue and Jeremy Senior goodbye, zipped up her hoodie, shouldered her pathetically small backpack and tried to stride off into the night like a confident and experienced hiker who definitely had a tent.

When they were around the corner, Claire paused to comment on how awkward the entire exchange had been.

'Probably some good clues, though, eh? Chin up,' said Soph.

They walked on in silence for a while, until Claire registered that she was colder than normal again. It was now dark, she realized. She had no extra clothes to put on, nothing to sleep in or on or under, a very low phone battery and, after using some of that battery to check, no bus home. She looked up. There were few street lights around, but unlike at The Cloisters, she couldn't see any stars. So, logically, that meant clouds, which meant there was a chance of rain.

She staggered a couple of steps, leaning all the way forward and then all the way back as she exhaled slowly.

'It's okay,' she said, as if she were reassuring Sophie, not herself. 'We'll just... we'll go back towards the pub we saw, right? That'll be open, probably.'

'That's... sensible of you.'

'I know,' said Claire proudly. 'So. Did you see anything in there?'

'Not more than you, really. Kevin's an only child, and they miss him. He really likes people. He makes friends easily.'

'Which is weird, because he is clearly quite annoying – from everything else we've heard,' added Claire. 'But... I hope it's not him. I mean, I hope it's not anyone. But I hope it's not him, for his mum's sake. Kevin's a spoilt "citizen of the world" type, but he's not, like, the *worst*. And Sue gave me hand-warmers.'

'LOL. In need of some motherly love, my little flower?' Sophie pretended to tickle her. Claire did not react, and stared into the dark.

'Well, it's got to be Mattie, right?' Sophie went on. 'Kevin is still in touch with his parents. I mean, I say "Kevin". The name thing is weird.'

'Not really,' said Claire. 'People get nicknames for loads of random reasons. I bet it went: Jerry, to Kevin & Jerry – like *Kevin & Perry Go Large* – to just Kevin. Rich kids like Figgy and Tris do that sort of shit all the time. "Eoooh, his name is Martin, but we all call him Jack, because once he puked up a whole bottle of Jack Daniel's at my sister's wedding, the fucking *ledge*." Don't you remember that guy everyone called Beard because one time he grew a beard for a bit? Or at uni, the kid called David, who got everyone to call him Michael because—'

'Because he really liked R.E.M. Ohmigod, yes. What a loser. On many levels.'

'Yeah. But yeah, you're right. Which means… that it's definitely Mattie, I suppose.'

'The one person we have almost no clues about. Fucksake.'

'Back to the drawing board.'

'Back to The Cloisters probably, if we really want to figure this all out.'

'I'm never going back there again,' said Claire, with some feeling. 'I'd either get shanked by Clem or disappeared by assassins that Monty hires through an offshore account.'

The pub was still open, but it didn't have rooms. Claire drank mulled cider until closing at eleven, mindful that the first few hours in a cold, unfeeling world would go more quickly if she was a bit pissed. She considered dipping into the blood-money that Hugh had sent, with every drink she bought, but couldn't quite bring herself to do it yet.

'Well,' said Sophie, as they left the pub and watched the other customers disappear back to their probably fully central-heated homes, 'since you're having all the good ideas today: where are we going to go now?'

17

Old-Time Religion

When she thought back on the totality of events, Claire would never be able to pinpoint exactly when she decided to try and break into a church – only that it seemed like a good idea at the time. But she was also drunk, so many things seemed like a good idea.

She had, for example, sort of forgotten that she didn't know how to pick locks, and had straightened a single hairpin and was trying to open the church door by sticking it in the lock and wiggling it around. She had definitely seen someone do this on *Murder Profile* and was feeling confident that she was actually quite good at it and was definitely catching at least one of the key pins inside the lock.

She had one ear pressed against the wood of the door, listening intently. There were several minutes of industrious silence.

'I think,' Soph said at last, as if talking to an animal she didn't want to spook – a rabbit, or an Englishman on holiday in Spain – 'that might be for cracking safes.'

'Think 's the wrong kind of lock anyway,' said Claire, unperturbed. 'I'm going to... gonna slice it with one of my cards. Where's my bag?'

'Let's maybe leave the bank cards as a back-up option,' said Soph.

Claire's idea to return to the church *had* been another good one, because the main entrance had a solid sort of porch that was paved and deep enough to have a stone alcove on either side of the door, with an inbuilt bench. It was enough for a medium-sized medium and/or an unprepared idiot to shelter in, for a few hours.

The problem was that the rain clouds had broken while they were still walking back. At first it was the kind of hesitant spit-spotting that made Claire wrap her coat a little closer around herself. But soon it became a proper deluge, the kind of rain that came down with a noise like the sea and shimmered across you in flapping curtains like billowing silk, but that stung when they whipped you in the face. By the time they got to the church, Claire was soaked to the skin, although she almost didn't notice.

Sophie had decided that it was best to get her inside as soon as possible. 'I bet someone comes in to help sometimes,' she said aloud. 'Some old lady doing the flower-arranging or, like, dusting the pulpit. There must be a spare key somewhere.'

Claire judged this to be sound. She bent over to look under the doormat, half fell over the weight of her own head and tumbled sideways into the door. She sat down, sneezed and started laughing.

Sophie scratched her head. 'Good impulse, weirdo. Lacking in execution. Stay there a second.'

Claire watched as Sophie walked through the door. She reached up and stroked the wood where her friend had disappeared. It was cold, but very solid. There were iron studs in it and everything.

Then she turned her head and looked out into the graveyard. It was very dark. She could barely see anything past the entrance to the porch. She was in a little lifeboat, she thought, or on a small island. And out there was the rain, her enemy. Sometimes it got in a bit, but it couldn't get in all the way. She'd been too clever for it. Ha-ha.

She became aware that the rain was flashing off something, out in the darkness. It was a little smudge of chalk on a blank slate. Claire beckoned at it, and it came closer and resolved into Luke, the little ghost boy from earlier.

''Lo,' she said.

''Lo,' he replied. 'I've been watching you.'

'Rude of you. Big rude-o.' She slumped her head back and closed her eyes, but that was bad, because everything was going a bit spinny. 'Where've you lot been?' she asked him. He shrugged in reply: they were around, or gone, or everywhere and nowhere. Where did they go when they weren't here? Who knew? Claire didn't. Maybe they went into the memory of the stones, in the graves, in the grass, in the ground.

'What's wrong with you then?' he asked.

'I had too much to drink.'

'Huh!' Luke managed to convey, in one syllable, the full force of an eleven-year-old's contempt for the adult condition. 'Did you go to my house then?'

Claire nodded and described what the upstairs bedroom looked like now.

Luke was stout of heart. 'S'pose lots of things have changed,' he said. 'S'pose the whole place is different now.'

'Footballs are better,' said Claire. 'All made of... something – something special for making good footballs anyway. And... and England won the World Cup in 1966.'

This visibly cheered Luke up. 'Well,' he said, 'Howard didn't say that. That's all right.'

Claire asked if there were spare keys to the church, and if he knew where they were. Luke considered the question, which Claire decided meant he *did* know. She waited.

'I s'pose it's all right if you go in,' he said eventually. 'If I go with you. You won't do anything to get me into trouble?' Claire pointed out that he was probably past the point of getting into trouble. Luke nodded and gestured to the eaves of the porch. 'Up there.'

Claire stood and felt along the ledge under the roof. Yes, keys! Excellent. There was one for the big old impressive lock, and one for the smaller modern one. The door was heavy. The creak when it opened and the clunk as she pushed it closed again was an alarm that surely alerted everyone within a five-mile radius.

Inside, the church smelled of cold stone and old wood. Claire could make out the first few pews and the pillars shooting up to the distant ceiling. She whistled into the space in front of her, but there was no echo, as if the sound was absorbed by an unseen listener. Sophie loomed out of the dark like the top tenth of an iceberg.

Claire realized she was shivering. The ghosts led her to a side room near the pulpit, where she guessed the vicar got psyched up before doing his sermons; she imagined him shadow-boxing like Rocky, and started laughing again. There was a wire-fronted electric heater and she turned it on. The filaments started glowing like a baleful eye, pumpkin-orange and with a demonic flavour that struck Claire as vaguely transgressive in a church. In its dim light she found two brass candlesticks and a box of sensible, white Church of England-compliant candles in a cupboard, and after some fumbling with her lighter she was holding one aloft like a trembling Edwardian widow. The trembling was literal, since the shivers had now completely overtaken her and she stood there in her soggy clothes, a little forlorn, in that delicate way people did when they were trying not to touch any part of themselves with any other part of themselves.

'Here, look,' said Sophie, pointing at a dark mass hanging on the back of the door. 'It's a robe-thingy. A cassock.' She made Luke turn round and encouraged Claire to change into it, arguing that if the vicar had been here, he would have insisted, because it was the most Christian thing to do; and if he hadn't insisted, then he wasn't a proper Christian and was actually a massive shit.

Claire peeled off her wet clothes. They stuck to her, especially her jeans, and she felt as if she was pulling off an old skin. She hung them off the back of a chair and, hands clumsy with cold and cider, positioned the heater so that maybe it would get the worst of the damp out of them.

Standing almost naked in a church made her feel sort of *extra* naked. It took a while getting the cassock on, because she kept mixing up the arm holes and the head hole. It was black and much too big for her, and she felt like a child dressing up. The material was some kind of scratchy polyester, but it was, to her benefit, completely dry. She did the universal 'Look how big this thing is on me' T-pose.

Sophie laughed affectionately at her. 'It's a good look,' she said. 'Strong look.'

Claire fished around in her bag. She found, to her dismay, that many of her Case Notes were soggy, because cheap canvas bags are not known for their waterproof qualities. With the exaggerated care of the drunk, she tipped most of them out and peeled apart some of the more damaged pages, laying them out flat on the floor with some reverence. She also located a lone cigarette rattling around in a fag packet, and got down a couple of grateful gasps of hot smoke before Soph started going on about fire alarms. *Yeah, yeah. It's fine. It's all made out of stone anyway.*

'D'you think God is cross?' Claire asked, her tongue feeling very thick in her mouth.

'If he exists, he's probably got enough complaints about you at this point,' said Sophie. 'I shouldn't worry.'

'I reckon he does exist,' Luke chipped in. 'Or why would we still be here?'

'Can't argue with that,' said Claire. 'S'logical. Although fingers crossed now that he doesn't, cos we've done like, *well* a blasphemy.'

Luke nodded, taking her quite seriously. He was sitting on top of the cupboard that she had previously relieved of candles, and was kicking his heels. It seemed he was determined to keep watch on her all night, to make sure she didn't vandalize his church.

Claire stumbled back out into the main bit – the big main part, with the sitting and standing and singing and all that: whatchacallit? She regarded the altar and the cross on it. It looked quite spooky in the dark.

'Wh-what's this all about then, eh? Why me? Why us? Whaddid we ever do to you?' she shouted, suddenly irritable. There was no response. 'Ha! But the ol' religion keeps her secrets, eh? Typical.'

She hadn't properly unpacked her bag for the whole week, so it still had all her seance kit inside it. After some thought, she went and retrieved her ornate old Bible, and put it with the others on the back of one of the pews. It was a lot bigger than all the rest. This pleased her. She put her candlestick in the cupboard in the vestry. Vestry! Good word. Well done for remembering it.

'You're going to regret that tomorrow,' said Sophie, who had been following Claire as she made her erratic, giggling progress around the church, to make sure she didn't break anything. 'You're going to have to buy some new ones now.'

Claire was now sitting on the floor and had wedged herself up against the bench, feet in front of the heater. It was actually doing a pretty good job of warming the room. She located her phone and was dimly pleased it wasn't wet. She swiped through some of the photos Alex had sent her from the party a year ago, until she came to one where Alex and Basher were smiling together in the foreground, and she smiled back at them. *Ah, Alex and Basher are nice.* It was the photo where Michael was in the background. He was talking to a dark-haired woman she didn't recognize.

'Hey. HEY! Sophie,' she said, holding the phone out unsteadily. 'Whozat?'

'Hold still... oh. That's Mattie, I think. Why?'

'She's wearing Tuppence's cardigan.'

'Hmm? Oh yes, she is. That's weird.'

Claire thought about this. The facts: Mattie had been selling family secrets. Then she disappeared. Her husband is embarrassed, and her son is weirded out, but nobody has reported her missing. Tuppence disappears in the house for unexplained stretches of time, is sharing a cardigan with Mattie and has filed for divorce. Claire started laughing very hard. She picked through her Case Notes with an idle finger and retrieved her newest piece of evidence: the photo of Kevin – except not Kevin, but Jerry.

'Hey, Luke,' she asked, head flopping back against the cushion on the bench. 'Hey, Luke. Luke. What's your last name?'

'Maguire,' he said.

'Ha-ha-ha! Fuck off. It is not.'

''Tis so.'

'Ha-ha-ha. Jerry Maguire!'

Sophie was watching her carefully.

Claire sat wiggling her toes at the evil eye of the heater. The rain was still hammering at the walls and windows, but she was inside now. In a big fort. Ha-ha. There was a broken gutter on the outside somewhere, and Claire could hear the violent splatter from where it was overflowing. It was rhythmical and comforting. It was out there, all wet. And she was in here, warming up her toesies, all full of cider and pheasant. Pheasant – like the dead ones. Argh. She could feel herself slipping into unconsciousness and forced her eyes open to look at the photo in her hand.

'Jerry Maguire,' she snorted. Why would he have such a stupid nickname when his name was already literally Jerry Maguire? That's a built-in joke! Some kind of 'you had me at hello' thing made more sense than a *Kevin & Perry* reference. Someone else had been talking about that, hadn't they? Hmm. She was very tired.

She looked at Kevin's smiling face. He looked so happy. She wondered where he was going. But something else in the picture was trying to get her attention. Her head was jangling at her again, like it had for beacon and bacon. What was it about the picture? It wasn't the guy Kevin was with. Who cared about him? Nobody. Never seen him before. Loser. Get out of the way, loser man. Not important.

338

Kevin was happy. He was about to fly somewhere. He was holding all his flying stuff – he'd printed out his boarding pass. He probably kept all of them, for some kind of boring scrapbook. But he was holding something else too, only the boarding pass was covering most of it. Something bright blue.

And suddenly she realized. She understood it all. It was all so clear and obvious.

'Soph! Sophie!' she shouted. At least she tried to shout, but it came out as a slur. She had to make Sophie understand. But her eyes had fallen shut again and they were so heavy. Ugh! 'Soph. Look. S'blue.'

'What?'

'Blue. The thing. He can't be gone.'

'Ohmigod, you weirdo. What are you talking about?'

'Ugh! *Listen*. The blue. *The blue!* Like the heater!' Why wasn't Sophie listening?

'The heater? The heater's orange, Claire. Look, explain again in the morning.'

Claire was frustrated. Why didn't Sophie understand? It wasn't that complicated. Her thoughts were getting crossed over, and she was very, very sleepy. But it was important that Soph understood. She tried one last time. 'We have to... We've got to go back, Soph. Got to... go.'

She couldn't hold on any longer. The photo dropped from her hand onto the floor. She could just about hear Sophie and Luke as she slipped into unconsciousness.

'To be honest, she wasn't making much less sense there than she does when she's sober,' Sophie remarked to Luke.

The two of them sat there, talking quietly as the candles burned down. After a few minutes Claire started snoring. Under the cold gaze of two dead children, she slept the unrestful sleep of the blackout.

Breakin' the Law

The next day started poorly and went downhill from there. Inasmuch as one can sleep in, while passed out in a church that one has broken into while drunk, Claire accidentally slept in. She woke with an almost entirely numb arse, curled up on the floor. She was woken by Sophie, who had progressed from talking in her ear, up through shouting, standing in her, and the last resort of actually shoving Claire a bit, which she wasn't supposed to do without permission.

'Don't panic,' said Sophie, causing Claire to panic immediately.

She found she was wrapped in great swathes of cassock, to such an extent that she fell over three times just trying to stand up. At some point in the night she had pulled all of her limbs inside it, like the world's saddest, yet most devout tortoise.

'I said *don't* panic, weirdo. Maybe a small amount of panic. There's a woman coming through the graves

– she'll be in the doorway in a couple of minutes. Go-go-go.'

'Go *where*?' hissed Claire. 'Oh Christ,' she said suddenly, as her movement caught up with her, 'Christ, I'm going to be sick.' The cider hangover was worse than the one she'd got from the group rager with Tris, or the second rager with Alex. She vaguely remembered shouting at God the night before and regretted it.

'Do *not* be sick,' ordered Sophie. 'There's a side door behind that curtain.'

Claire stuffed all her errant bits of paper and mostly dry clothes into her bag, shoved the burnt-out candles in their holders back into the cupboard, and was flicking the off-switch on the heater just as the clanking sound of the main door echoed into the nave. She slipped out of the promised side door, which, luckily, had a latch lock. She caught it at the last second, remembering to leave the keys on the side table, and closed it as silently as possible. It was the worst Indiana Jones moment of all time.

Sophie walked along at a sedate pace as Claire crouch-ran through the graves, clutching her half-zipped rucksack to her front, and did a kind of lopsided attempt at a barrel roll into the bushes at the back of the graveyard. She poked her head out cautiously and noted that she had an audience. The church ghosts were watching. Maisie paused long enough to make it clear she was taking the piss and then waved. Sophie stopped to chat to them for a moment, and then sauntered over with a distinct lack of urgency.

Claire ducked down and was extremely sick onto the ground. *Vintage teenage vomming*, she thought. *Throwing up in a graveyard after drinking too much cider: absolute classic.* Could only be improved if it had been cans of Strongbow. She wondered if the police had vom experts, like they did for fingerprints. Could this puke tie her to the scene of her crime? It wasn't much of a crime, though. She hadn't technically broken in, and had only lightly used some candles.

Oh, she'd stolen a spare cassock, hadn't she? But stealing clothes off washing lines and what-have-you was, like, a cheery lovable crime, such as someone like Billy Elliot would do. Claire flopped back onto the dirt, still somehow exhausted.

'Why didn't you wake me sooner?' she grumbled, as Sophie finally arrived.

'*Ohmigod*. I don't have a watch, do I? Don't have anything. How do I know what time it is? Anyway it seemed like you needed to sleep it off.' Sophie surveyed her with a critical eye. 'I think you might be sick, you know. Did that feel like a hangover yak-up or, like, an "I'm actually dying" yak-up?'

'Dunno. I suppose only time will tell.' Claire put her hand to her forehead. It felt hot, but she was not sure if this was because her hand was cold or not. She remembered her mum putting her hand on her forehead when she'd been sick as a child, but she wasn't sure what kind of arcane knowledge was divined from this. It wasn't like she or her mum had thermometers instead of fingers.

By half crouching, half crab-crawling through the sparse hedgerows, Claire (who now thought of herself as being on the run, at least until she made it back to civilization, i.e. somewhere with colour-coded train lines) remained inconspicuous on the way back to the bus stop – although really because it was after 8 a.m. on a weekday and nobody was looking. Aware that she was still cosplaying a vicar, and because it was starting to spit rain again, she stood inside the phone box, breathing slowly and concentrating on not being sick again.

She looked at the phone and remembered something.

'Soph?' she asked, trying not to move in case it dislodged more hangover.

'Mmm?'

'You know when you asked if Monty's firm used Samsungs? Why did you ask that?'

'Because Tristan has two iPhones.'

'Yeah. Hmm.'

'Is this something to do with what you were on about last night? The blue and the heater?'

'What? Oh. *OH!*' Claire suddenly remembered. The rudeness and the urgency of the remembrance made her snap her head up, and she whacked the back of it against one of the panes of the phone box. 'OW! Fucksticks!'

'LOL. That knock anything loose?'

'Yes! Sort of. I figured it out, Sophie! I know what happened. Or...' she faltered, 'I *knew*. I definitely *did*. I can't remember all of it right now, but I saw it all last night. Argh.' She rubbed her head. Her brain was now

344

being assaulted by pain from without and within. 'Shit! If I just had an hour to myself I could remember it all. I'm sure I could.'

Sophie looked sceptical. 'Do you remember the main thrust?'

'Yes. I think so. We need to go back to The Cloisters. Like, right now.'

'That seems like a bad idea. You said you never wanted to go back.'

'I don't. But – not to be mean – it's not like you can stop me, is it?'

'The funeral is today,' Soph pointed out, in a tone that indicated this was another reason to stay away.

'Yeah, but that means they'll be out of the house most of the day,' said Claire. 'Plus, Bash and Alex will definitely be there, so if we get caught, they can, like... stop me being murdered.'

'Caught,' asked Soph, responding perfectly to her feed-line, 'doing what?'

Claire took a deep breath. 'Caught breaking into The Cloisters.'

'And why are we going to do that?'

'Because I know who the ghost is. And I know how we can prove it.'

She was disappointed that the bus to the train station didn't round the corner at that very moment. They were waiting for another twenty minutes.

*

To get to Wilbourne Major they had to catch the bus back to Swindon and then the train into London, only to get a train back out again immediately from the other side of town. It was one of the most hellish tests of moral fibre that Claire had ever gone through. Each awkward turn on the bus was a fresh assault of nausea. Sophie was peppering her with questions, but she screwed her eyes shut and retreated into herself to find any atoms – any molecules within the entity that was Claire – that did not feel unwell, and tried to become them entirely.

At Swindon she took out some cash, and bought a phone charger and a bottle of sugary iced tea. The train tickets would take her almost to her overdraft limit, but she thought it would be worth it. On the train to London she plugged her phone in and looked up a couple of Instagram accounts. She nodded to herself in satisfaction. Sophie was growing impatient and stroppy, but Claire told her she needed to think. She got out some of the Case Notes and put them on the table in front of her. She tried to fit the pieces together as clearly as she had seen them the night before, but she felt them shimmering and changing shape if she looked at them too closely.

She would not remember getting across London. Sophie blew into her hot face and pressed her hands close, helped steer Claire through the thick, sticky veins of the Underground. On the train from London, Claire slept, and the fever set in, in earnest.

She had strange dreams. Dead pheasants with lolling heads and bright blue-and-white eyes. Monty and Ted the gardener were turning over potatoes with garden forks, but when she looked in the ground, they were burying Sophie. She tried to get them to stop, but Sophie opened her eyes and said it was all right. Claire looked up, and Ted and Monty had been replaced by the monk, who was still pointing. She ran into the house and saw Basher seated in front of the fire in the kitchen. He turned into an octopus and squeezed underneath the kitchen door, except that she knew it was the door to the library and she didn't want to go in, because she knew what was in there.

In the end, it was Sophie who roused her.

They had reached Wilbourne Major. It was early afternoon. Claire wasn't sure how long they'd have. She staggered down onto the platform and saw a sticker with a taxi company's number on the station sign. She tried calling it and then remembered there was no signal. Obviously. But a less-confused Claire had prepared for this at Swindon. She walked until she found a pay phone, this time at an intersection, and used some of the change from her iced tea and asked for someone to take her to the Red Line.

The driver, when he arrived, was alarmed. By this point, so was Sophie. Claire was pale and covered in cold sweat, but there was a strange glint in her eye that was terrible to behold. For her part, Claire was possessed of a kind of certainty that she had never felt before in her entire life.

'Why're we going to the pub instead of the house?' Sophie asked. 'That would be way easier.'

'Want to be as low-key as possible, though,' said Claire. 'Sneaky. Turning up at their front door in a taxi isn't very incognito. The house is only over the fields that way. Can easily walk.'

'I see the logic, but you wanting to walk anywhere is very out of character.'

The Red Line was full of people. Smokers were spilling out of the front door. They were all in black, so Claire, who had not bothered to change out of her cassock (although she had put her jeans on underneath, and her black hoodie on over the top) would at least fit in.

Oh, wait. Oh dear.

Peering through the window revealed people eating tiny cheese quiches, limp salad and tiny pieces of meat on tiny pieces of toast. Claire had hoped that if she ended up crashing the funeral, it would have been at the actual funeral, and she would have been standing in the graveyard at a distance, in mysterious Audrey Hepburn sunglasses rather than a second-hand stolen clerical robe. Tuppence was in the corner with Alex and Basher, who were standing close to one another, talking with their heads together. Her wasted heart thudded, and she almost lost grip of the iron rod of certainty that she would imminently use to batter down the door to the truth. So Claire turned away from the window. She put her hood up, in case any of the other Wellington-Forges were nearby.

Near the door she saw a familiar dog being held by a familiar figure. After a moment of hesitation, and with

Sophie hissing, 'What are you *doing?*' in her ear, Claire went over and bent down to stroke it. It was unbelievably soft. She buried her face in the fur and then stood up, unsteadily.

'Hello, Alf. I don't know if you remember me. I just wanted to say: I'm sorry. Like, I'm really fucking sorry. I was very rude to you before. I didn't mean to be.'

Alf assessed her, then nodded. 'Hmph. No harm done.'

'So,' said Claire, checking another hunch, 'Hugh's son once said that he isn't a good shot. Is he?'

Alf chuckled, despite himself. 'I'd say not, no.'

'And yet he always manages to hit loads of pheasants on shoots?'

Alf looked at her out of the corner of his eye and smiled in an almost bashful way, but didn't say anything.

'Say no more, Alf, say no more,' said Claire, as Sophie made an '*oh*' of understanding. 'Anyway, we must be off! Got a bit of a walk.' And she cheerily waved goodbye.

They hiked over the fields to The Cloisters, keeping off the road and the long drive, in case any of the family returned to the house unexpectedly. It was starting to rain again, but Claire couldn't feel it; in fact it felt like she was impervious to her old enemy, the sky-water, as if it hissed when it hit her skin. Sophie orbited Claire like a nervous moon. Claire tried to reassure her.

'It's okay, Soph. I know what I'm doing. This is really good actually. A finale! On the day of a fucking funeral! Just like on TV, like you said.'

Sophie didn't seem reassured.

349

Claire began to get tired. She started chanting Sophie's misremembered Spice Girls lyrics like a kind of incantation: Ham your shoddy clown and wipe it up and down. Over again, in march step. One foot in front of the other. Ham your shoddy clown and wipe it up and down. Eventually Sophie joined in. When the house came into view, it was getting dark and she looked more relieved than Claire.

Claire felt her knees begin to buckle, but she knew she could not stop, not for a moment. There could be no pause. It had to be as smooth as possible, because if she snagged on anything, she would unravel.

There were no lights on, and no signs of movement. They went round the back of the house, which was totally silent. Claire rattled the kitchen door as she passed, but it was locked. 'Key under the mat?' said Sophie hopefully – but Claire had already moved on, stalking to the other end of the building and the damp, sad rose garden. Ted was sitting there.

'Hello, Ted,' said Claire. She scooped up a big flinty stone from one of the flower beds.

'Miss Claire, is it? And Miss Sophie! Blimey. What're you two doing back here? I was just sitting here remembering Miss Janey.'

'That's nice, Ted,' said Claire dreamily. Then she turned and hoofed the stone as hard as she could at the library window.

Sophie threw up her hands. '*Ohmigod!* She's lost it, Ted! I can't stop her. This is it. Endgame. We're going to go to prison.'

The little panes shattered beautifully, all bulging inwards. Claire used her backpack to push as much of the rest of the glass through as possible, before hauling herself inside – she didn't want to be unsafe, after all. But she was mostly shrouded by the fabric of the cassock anyway. She dropped into the dark room like a crow with two broken wings and shook herself down. Ted and Sophie followed closely.

The ghost was there, on its hands and knees, crawling pathetically and mewling, scrabbling at the floor. A whole year spent like this.

Strangely, this time she felt no fear. Only sadness. And anger.

Claire dropped to her knees and reached out to the bony shoulders. She could feel a strange solidity, as if ghostly flesh still covered them, though her eyes could only see a few decaying wet ribbons of muscle and sinew. But she could feel the *zip* like she did with Sophie, and it was twice the drain now, because she had half the strength. 'But I have enough,' she whispered to herself. She made herself look the ghost in the face, as she forced it to experience her presence.

'I'm going to help you,' she said. 'I'm going to find you. Hold on, okay? Just a little bit more. Fuck, I know it's hard. But you can do it. Just a little more. We can do it.'

This seemed to calm the ghost. Claire hauled herself to her feet and it stood as well. It was still. She felt the ghost's gaze on her as she walked as quickly as she could out of the library and into the strange maze of the house.

'Which way is the office?' she asked.

'This way,' said Sophie and Ted together.

The office door was unlocked. Claire did not have a plan, physically or mentally, for if it had been locked. She went straight to the desk drawer and pulled it open.

'Oh, thank God.' She nearly wept with relief. 'It's still here. It's still here. They didn't get rid of it.' She reached in and picked up the thin notebook, with the blue cover decorated with what she now knew was the evil eye.

'Oh,' said Sophie. A light of understanding was starting to bloom in her face. 'Oh no.'

Claire opened it and turned to the last page. She nodded to herself once more. At that moment there was the slippery crunch of a car braking hard on wet gravel. 'Ah yes,' said Claire cheerily, as if she had factored this in. 'Probably a silent alarm.' She tucked the little booklet into her pocket as Sophie began directing her: the quickest way out is via the kitchen, so out to the kitchen we go, my girl.

There was a plate of drumsticks under cling film on the side.

'Why is it always fucking chicken?' murmured Claire. She paused to unwrap the plate and take a huge bite. *Ha-ha-ha, I am the chicken weirdo now, Clementine*, she thought; *I have cucked you in your own kitchen. Clucked you. Because, chicken.*

This lame standup bit to the inside of her own head proved to be Claire's undoing. The door onto the lawns swung open and the light flicked on, blinding her for a moment. She raised an arm to block the light, and in that same split second there was a blood-curdling scream of 'The monk! The *mooooonk!*' and a crash.

Claire realized that whoever had just opened the door had seen, in broad strokes, a figure in a black-hooded robe on the day of their grandmother's funeral. As the family legend foretold, a ghostly monk would appear to whomever of the family was next to die. That the detail in this case included sick-stains and a chicken drumstick was immaterial.

'It's Figgy!' Sophie yelled. 'She's keeled over in the doorway. Some others are with her. Let's go-go-*go!* This way.'

Claire obeyed instinctively; it was a voice she had been following almost all her life. She scrambled back the way she had come, following the bright jewel colours of Sophie's hair and clothes through the dark house. Behind them, she heard Figgy shouting something panicky.

'It was *not* the monk, Figgy,' came Monty's voice, deep and cold and dangerous as a glacial spring. 'It had trainers on.'

Sophie brought Claire back to the library and suddenly jinked to one side. Claire dived after her without pause and crashed straight into a bookshelf. She cracked her knees on the floor and grazed a hand, and suddenly everything was awful. It was like something had been uncorked in her throat and she started crying.

Sophie reappeared. 'Shhh,' she cooed. 'Shh, come on, love, it's okay. It's the priest-hole. Come on, quickly.'

Claire scrabbled to locate the button, and then crawled inside to the safety of the darkness. She clapped a hand over her mouth, so that she was crying in silence. Sophie went out to look.

Several pairs of footsteps thundered across the wooden floor, then came to a halt.

'Oh *no*, look. The window!' It was Clementine.

'It was her. I'm sure it was her.' There was Monty, spitting venom. 'That *bloody* woman.'

'D'you think she knows?' That was Tristan.

'Of course she bloody knows!' exploded Monty. 'Why else would she be here? For fuck's sake!'

'Don't worry, darling,' purred Clementine. 'Monty knows it was an accident, don't you, Monty?'

'It was that bloody ha-ha thing.' Tristan sounded like a petulant teenager who'd been asked why his homework wasn't finished. 'It's basically *your* fault, Mum. I told you and Dad there should be more lights out there.'

More facts slotted into place as Claire listened, fixed points in the churning, confused maelstrom of her thoughts.

The floorboards creaked as the footsteps moved around the room.

'She must have gone out into the grounds,' said Monty. '*You* need to get out there and find her – this whole thing is because of you.'

'I'm not going out there without a mac and some wellies,' moaned Tristan. The footsteps came closer to the priest-hole. She could hear someone breathing.

'Stay very still,' came Sophie's voice.

354

Then, very suddenly, there was a long, low wail, a scream, a crash and the sound of running feet. Then, silence.

'Quick! They've gone! The button works from the inside.'

Claire fell out of the priest-hole and lay on the floor, sobbing dry, ragged sobs. She raised her head and saw that the skeleton was lying on the floor too, giving a long, wordless moan. It must have appeared to the Wellington-Forges in order to save her. It had clearly cost a lot.

'Come on, get up,' said Sophie.

'I can't, I can't,' she cried.

'They're coming back, Claire!'

'It hurts,' Claire said, rolling over pathetically.

'Yeah, well, they say life is pain. Maybe that's how you know you're alive.'

'That's the stupidest fucking thing I've ever heard,' said Claire.

She looked at the skeleton again. She got up.

Grave Business

Claire had never understood the phrase 'my soul is about to leave my body' before, but as she sprinted across the lawn with the very last screed of energy within her, she did begin to feel strangely weightless. The icy air seemed to be forming cold diamonds in her lungs, so she was drawing less and less breath with every gasp. And now it was raining properly too, so her face was wet and the cassock was cloying, wrapping around her legs. It was like drowning on dry land.

The burning of the lungs in her chest was matched by the burning of the lactic acid in her thighs and the bile rising in her throat. She was either going to pass out or throw up – except she could not do either, because the echoing shouts behind her were a reminder that she was being chased.

She laughed at the absurdity, but no sound came out, because she was already heaving air in and out of her lungs like a bellowing racehorse – albeit one with reduced lung capacity, from an entrenched smoking habit and what she was now realizing was probably the flu. Her heart was hammering too fast; it would surely explode. *This is how I die*, she thought. Record scratch. Freeze-frame. Yup, that's me.

Her rucksack was thumping against her arse in a very annoying way. It shouldn't have been important, but in that moment it really felt like it was.

It was almost pitch-black outside. Sophie was in front of Claire, calling out which way to go. Ted was beside her, pushing her forward with his usual unceasing muttering, though now it was gently encouraging: 'Come on, Miss Claire, nearly there – them toffs won't catch us, don't you worry...'

Suddenly Sophie yelled, 'Stop!' and they screeched to a halt, which was almost as painful as it would have been to keep running. 'It's the bloody pissing fucking ha-ha,' she said. 'It's just in front of you.'

Claire began to inch forward with some caution, having a wary respect for the ha-ha, but suddenly Ted shouted too. 'The lights!' he said. 'Miss, they're turnin' on the lawn lights.'

She spun round and saw that The Cloisters was now eerily lit by blueish floodlights pointing upwards from the ground, angled at the walls – the sort of thing to make the grey stone look good in wedding photos. The next step, then, would be floodlights on the building and the roof, angled at the grounds...

Claire panicked and took a blind running jump into the dark void in front of her.

It wasn't quite far enough. One foot clipped the top edge of the ha-ha's wall and pitched her forward. Something in her ankle *crunched*. She fell awkwardly at the bottom of the ditch and curled over like a child, biting her own hand to stop herself crying out at the pain, the white-hot red feeling blooming from her foot. She would have been winded if she wasn't already almost completely out of breath.

But she'd dropped out of sight before the lights hit her. The bright white of the lawn floodlights was blaring out over the top of the ha-ha, a big fanfare of the Wellington-Forges' reach. It cast a long shadow onto the rough grass beyond the lawn. But in the lee of the ha-ha, she was safe and hidden. They had no idea where she was. Claire took some satisfaction from that. Where once the rain and the dark were her enemies, now they were allies against the light. *Yes*, she thought to herself, as she began to hop along the length of the ditch, leaning on the rough bricks in lieu of a crutch, *I must become the dark...*

The ghosts followed her. Ted was walking along the top of the wall, keeping an eye out. 'Why's she doing a funny voice?' he asked Sophie eventually.

'Er...' said Sophie, who was walking alongside Claire, and apparently could not think of a way to explain the memetic qualities of certain movie characters to a long-dead gardener.

'You merely *adopted* the darkness...' mumbled Claire, unaware that they were talking at all, much less about her. They hobbled on for a few more minutes, although her perception of time was beginning to rubber-band in and out. It stretched to a point of agony, where each step felt like an hour, and then snapped back to her, so that she was aware she did not have enough of it and that every second was precious. If she could get to the far edge of the grass, she'd be in with a chance. From there, she thought, trying to remember the old blueprints, she could crawl along and make it around the hook-shaped bit of grass that reached to the back of the copse, where the old monastery ruins were. Claire was convinced that was where the body was. And if not, she could hide there. It'd be all right. She was quite warm now, really.

They were in sight of the bushes and scrubby trees that marked the right-hand boundary when Ted flapped his hands and indicated for them to be quiet. He even started whispering, which Claire thought was quite sweet. Sophie made a zip-yer-mouth-shut motion at Claire, because she was still muttering things like 'I didn't see the light until I was already a man.'

Footsteps were slipping over the wet grass. Claire pressed up flat against the wall, trying to disappear into it, if at all possible. Her breathing was still ragged and she tried to hold it in, but she was pretty sure it wouldn't matter, because they'd hear the pounding of her heart and the thunderous rushing of her blood.

The lights of a couple of powerful torches were tracking back and forth across the distant trees of the copse, but without much enthusiasm. And they were very narrow beams, lighting up only what they were shining on directly. That was good to know.

'I don't... I don't fucking like it, Monty,' said Tristan, who now sounded like he was, or was about to start, crying. 'It's fucked – the whole thing is fucking fucked.'

'Everything will be *fine* once we find her,' replied Monty, doing a very good job of sounding confident. They were both half shouting over the rising wind.

'You saw it too, Monters. What the fuck was that – it wasn't a fucking monk, it's after me, Monty, what are we going to do?'

'Shut up. Just shut up. We didn't see anything.'

The torches flicked off. Footsteps turned away, back towards the house.

'Don't say anything in front of Alex or Basher, you bloody idiot, you know that they'll...' But then they trailed out of earshot.

Ha-ha, thought Claire. I was right under their noses, and they didn't even know. Good ol' cassock. Good ol' darkness.

After a moment Ted indicated they should move again. 'You all right, Miss Claire?' he asked.

Claire smiled cheerfully at him. '"The shadows betray *you*, because they belong to me!"'

'I think that's a yes,' said Sophie critically. 'I don't think we have a choice any more, anyway.'

'My foot hurts,' Claire added. 'This thing is a health-and-safety nightmare. Tristan *did* fall over and ruin his suit, and he *did* get in a fight, but that's not the whole story, you see? If you want to lie well, you tell a bit of the truth.'

'That's making more sense. Attagirl.'

'Oh yes, that's exactly what happened. I saw the whole thing,' said Ted, as if he wasn't saying anything at all. Claire stopped and looked at him incredulously.

'You saw the whole thing? This whole time?'

'The fight last year, and the body and that? Of course. Lot of us did. Not much interesting goes on round here. Someone gets killed, we all has a look. You would too.' Claire started laughing uncontrollably, until Sophie shushed her.

'Ohmigod, Ted,' said Soph, turning on the old man. 'Why didn't you *say*?'

'You never asked!' said Ted, sounding affronted. 'How'm I s'posed to know what you want to know and what you don't, of everything that happens here? And you all buggered off after a day.'

'Bloody hell,' grumbled Sophie as they reached the end of the ha-ha.

Claire got on all fours and crawled into the bushes and leaf mould. It already smelled of death. Also, of what she suspected was sheep shit. She fumbled into her pocket for Sophie's hair-clip to rub at, for comfort, but it wasn't there. She started thrusting her hands into the dead leaves and dirt in a panic, trying to find it, but she was mindful that Tristan would soon be back out, with his torch and his wellies.

'What are you doing, idiot?' said Sophie. 'Come on – come the fuck on!'

Claire got up and started to limp/hop/run towards the ruins. She glanced back towards The Cloisters and saw pale figures drifting across the lawn. Evidently Ted was right. The local ghosts turned out for anything exciting. But as she looked, the kitchen door opened again and disgorged a hunting party of Wellington-Forges. Claire didn't pause to count them, but hobbled off into the darkness once more. The wet slick of leaves made a terrible noise as she dragged her feet through them, but she couldn't be sure that it wasn't lost in the wind anyway.

With directions from Ted, they made it to the ruins. These were suddenly cast into sharp monochrome relief by a crackle of lightning – the first appropriately dramatic moment of the night. Claire approved.

She hadn't expected the ruins to be so... ruinous. The tallest point was the shell of a two-storey building, but it clearly was no more than that – it had no guts or roof left. There were vestiges of walls for other structures, and two and a half rows of columns forming part of a square, some of them broken and sticking up like jagged teeth. The titular cloisters.

'Come on,' Sophie encouraged her. 'In here.' She pointed Claire to the building.

As she got close, she could make out that it was made of stone in all different sizes, no nice clean uniform bricks. It was almost like it was formed of a single lump of clay. As Claire stepped towards the blank gap of the doorway, a tall figure loomed into it.

'Argh! Christ! Don't do that!' she exclaimed.

It was the monk. *The* Monk. Simeon, Ted had called him. She'd seen him the very first day, but far off. Up close,

Claire could see why he would frighten a lot of people, possibly to death. He was very tall, and all you could see under his cowl was a stern mouth and a long, thin nose, the same colour as his cloudy grey habit. He stood there, looking imposing, sizing her up. Around him the rain pounded on the walls of his home, yet he stood implacable. Calm as the stones. Claire felt small and ashamed, and wanted to apologize that anyone had ever mistaken her for him, even if only for a second. And for all the blasphemy.

When Simeon spoke, his voice was deep and rich, and he had no need to shout against the wind.

''Sup,' he intoned.

'I... Sorry, what?'

'It is a traditional greeting, is it not?'

'LOL!' said Sophie.

It was her first LOL in a while, and hearing it calmed Claire down a bit. Her foot was throbbing in a way that indicated rubbing it and going 'ooooh, owwww' for a bit wasn't going to cut it; her skin was sizzling; her thoughts were flying into all corners of her head like frozen peas sliding under the cooker, and she was very, very afraid. But Sophie could still do a LOL. So it wasn't all bad.

'This way, child,' said Simeon, stepping aside and sweeping out a proprietary arm. 'He is here.'

Claire staggered into the shadow of the building. The rain still swept in, but the sound and fury of the wind were immediately less. She decided to chance the torch on her phone. 'Can't see fuck all otherwise,' she explained out loud.

Simeon coughed in disapproval, but otherwise stayed silent.

It was a sad little room. The floor was bare mud, with puddles here and there and leaves building up in drifts in the corners. There was a patchy carpet of sickly green moss and little stones, but Claire thought – perhaps imagined – that one area was disturbed and wasn't as weathered as the rest. She noticed a spade, starting to grow rusty, discarded to one side. Immaterial. Doesn't matter. Leave it all here.

'You tried to show me, didn't you?' she said suddenly, looking up at Simeon. In reply, he only spread his hands in mute appeal. 'Bloody ghosts! Why can't you ever *say* what you want. It's all cryptic this, and pink shepherdesses that! Oh don't mind me, I'll just pick up the shovel, will I? Yes, I will. Fucksake. Can't even hold the torch for me. Go and keep a lookout, Ted.'

'You're sounding more lucid,' remarked Sophie.

'Well, I'm narked off, aren't I?' she replied.

Claire began to dig. It was very hard because the earth was cold, and she couldn't put her weight on her bad foot either, to leverage the shovel, or to push down on it. She started jumping awkwardly on the blade with her good foot and levering it with her whole body. Clods of earth began to come up. Claire was exhausted. Her arms were like noodles.

More ghosts were seeping through the walls as she worked. All ages, all epochs, shapes and sizes. The air grew unbearably cold. The rain falling inside the walls turned to sleet and then snow. It was, Claire thought, almost beautiful. She fell to her knees and started using the shovel with her hands, holding it near the top of the blade and dragging and scraping away at the ground. Her fingers were numb. The exertion was throwing iron rings around her heart and chest again. She could not breathe deeply enough. She was sobbing out loud in rage and pain and fear, but she couldn't feel the tears.

At last the point of the blade hooked on something. A loop of plasticky canvas material. It wasn't really very deep after all. Of course it wasn't. They didn't even care *that* much. Claire grabbed it and pulled, and the ground disgorged it, almost vomited it up like it knew it shouldn't be there. It was a backpack. A proper one. Covered in patches and badges. COEXIST. She set it to one side and saw that it had brought something else with it.

It was still half buried, but it gleamed yellowish-brown in the light of her phone: an almost skeletonized arm, from the elbow down. Claire was dimly aware that if she'd been in a normal state of mind she would have been horrified. But now she felt only relief. She reached out shakily and clasped the hand.

'Hey, Jerry,' she said. 'I've got you. Your mum misses you. I've got you.'

Several things happened. First, Claire heard someone shouting. Second, she felt the lifting of a great oppressive weight that she hadn't even realized was pushing down on her. This was tempered a bit by the third event, which was an explosion of agony from her injured foot, because someone was using it to pull her back.

She slid over the muddy ground. Her rucksack was pulled off her back, twisting her arms round as it went. She screamed a gargling, unwilling scream of pure pain and kicked out instinctively with the other leg. It caught someone in the arm and they fell back: Tristan, who dropped his torch. It lit him from below and he looked haggard and scared. His face was streaked with tears.

'Tris!' Claire cried desperately. 'Please, Tris, it's okay. I know it wasn't your fault.' He hesitated and looked confused. Claire pressed on. The wind was quieter in here, so she lowered her voice and talked calmly. 'It's okay. You'd just fought about the Arrowhead Beacon thing, right? You were trying to protect the firm – to make Monty proud. And Kevin fell off the wall in the dark. You weren't to know. He hit his head on a rock – you didn't kill him. It could have happened to anyone.'

Tristan nodded almost involuntarily and picked up his torch slowly. Sophie nodded too. 'You've got him Claire, you've got his number. Exactly like a seance. You know what to do.'

'That's what I thought. I bet it was your mum who made you cover it up, wasn't it? They put so much pressure on you, but it's not your fault—'

Other people were shouting in the distance now, and Tristan's head snapped round.

'No, Tristan, wait, please, you don't have to... aaa*rrghaaaaa*!'

He pulled on her foot again and shouted, 'Here! She's here! I've got her for you, Monty!'

Sophie stepped forward so that she was occupying the same space as Tristan. He did an involuntary full-body spasm, and Claire managed to kick out with her good leg again. She cracked him across the face as he bent over; he landed with a thump and did not immediately get up again. His torch fell and winked out.

Claire scrabbled to her feet, but her phone had skittered off and the light was gone. There was only the wild disco-swinging of someone else's torch, and she couldn't see – she couldn't see! Someone slapped her across the face, hard, and she fell down again.

'Sophie!' she screamed. 'Sophie, where are you?' She was so afraid. She had never been alone. She started crying again, but in a desperate way, like a child.

'You're mad,' said a familiar, cruel voice, full of contempt. 'But at least that means nobody will believe you.'

Stupid, stupid Claire. What was the plan, anyway? Dig up a dead body in the middle of the night, and then what? Hike back towards the pub and die in the field on the way there? Ask the Wellington-Forges, very nicely, if she could use their phone to snitch on them? She rolled over, mewling.

Ted was raging at Monty. 'Bastard! You toffee-nosed bastard! You're a disgrace.' He was flailing and punching right through Monty's face, but all it did was cause Monty to shiver and twitch his nose. Claire could see the other ghosts watching. The Monk was bending over to look at Tristan.

'Sophie?' she whispered.

At last: 'I'm here. I'm right here. I'm not going anywhere.'

'Sophie, I can't get up,' Claire sobbed.

'You will,' said Sophie firmly. 'You fucking *will*. You will, because nobody else here can. I can't. I'm not strong enough. I need you to do it for me. Please, Claire. You were always stronger than me.'

'I can't, Soph, I can't. I'm not strong. I don't have anything left. Please tell me it's okay to stop.'

'If that's what you really want, you can stop. I'll hold your hand and you can go to sleep. But I don't think you want that yet.'

'But I'm so tired. It hurts. I lost your hair-clip, Sophie. I dropped it somewhere out there.'

'That doesn't matter. It's only a thing. It's not real. It doesn't matter,' said Sophie. 'I'm not real, Claire. It doesn't matter.'

Claire realized that Sophie was crying too. She hadn't ever seen Sophie cry. Her tears disappeared before they hit the ground. 'I can't do it alone,' she whispered.

'You're not alone. Let's do it all together, Miss Claire,' said Ted, stepping away from Monty. His voice was quiet and firm, like he knew exactly what to do. 'All of us together, eh, Miss Sophie?'

'I don't know how,' said Sophie, equally quietly. 'It only takes. When I hold her it only takes from her.'

'Ah, it won't be that hard. Don't take, Miss Sophie. Push the other way. We can help you give.' He reached out his hand to Sophie and she, after some hesitation, took it.

And, smiling and kind, with his other hand Ted beckoned to the other ghosts. 'Don't just stand there looking, you useless buggers.'

Slowly, but then with more confidence, the dead of The Cloisters linked hands. Simeon first, and then the old lady and the little Frenchman, still bickering. A girl in a sailor dress and a straw boater. A serious-looking butler. On and on through the centuries, a daisy chain of the dead. Claire could not understand what was happening.

Monty, without the distraction of a cold ghost slapping him in the face, was advancing on Claire. He looked wild. His hair was askew, his suit was torn. He was, she was sure, probably going to kill her. Claire heard more shouting, saw more flickering light in the distance. She hauled herself back a few feet, met her rucksack, scrabbled in it for her candlestick to use as a weapon and then realized she no longer had it. Monty laughed at her, and she saw how pathetic she must look in his eyes.

Then Sophie took her hand.

A river of warmth flowed into Claire. Strength flowed down hundreds of years, from one memory of life to the next and the next, pouring their existence through Sophie, and through Sophie into Claire.

'Get up, weirdo. Get up one last time. *Get. Up.*'

Claire rose like an avenging angel. There was no pain. There was no fog clouding her mind. Even if she wasn't actually glowing, she *felt* like she was. She felt like stars sparkled in the wake of her every movement. She felt like death astride a pale horse. And she did have a weapon.

Her arm swung in a graceful parabolic arc as she strode forward, backed by the vengeful dead of every generation. She hit Monty with great and terrible force, full across the face, with a big purple dildo.

He spun. He frowned. He dropped. Cold-cocked.

Claire let go of Sophie's hand and stood, swaying, as she lost herself again. One by one, the ghosts were disappearing. The snow was turning back into rain. Soon it would all be gone, like nothing had happened. She saw Ted smile and blow a kiss as he faded away, and she tried, groggily, to reach out to him. Her vision dimmed and she staggered sideways as she began, at last, to faint. It was probably long overdue. The last thing she saw as she fell was Basher sprinting towards her, and the last thing she heard was Sophie screaming.

'Help her. Fucking *help her*!'

20

After the Funeral

The next thing Claire knew was a white ceiling. There was pain in her foot, but it was remote. She observed the sensation objectively, like it was happening to someone else. Mmm. That was a hurty ankle all right.

Good deduction. Back on track.

She turned her head to one side and further observed that she could only blink very slowly. There was a machine bleeping at her, and a drip-thingy. Stuck in her arm. Furthermore, the wall was a curtain, and Sophie wasn't there.

'Sfr?' she said.

'LOL. This side, weirdo.'

She rolled her head to the other side. Sophie was lolling in a chair that had wooden arms and upholstery that looked easy to wipe down. A nurse in an old-time sixties uniform was standing next to her.

'Whermy?'

Sophie opened her mouth, but was cut off.

'You're in the Royal Bournemouth Hospital,' said the nurse. 'And you gave everyone a fright, I'm sure. Now, you just go back to sleep. We've got you on plenty of fluids and a good whack of painkillers. You need to rest up and let your body heal. Keep you in for a week, I shouldn't wonder! Now I must do the rest of my rounds.'

She breezed through the other dividing curtain in a chilly gust. Soph jerked her head after her. 'Ohmigod. Thought she'd never leave. Barrel of laughs, her. And FYI, I heard a more this-century nurse say they'd probably hoof you out tomorrow, if not later today. NHS cutbacks, mate. They need the beds, and you've been sleeping it off for a night already. I'm very bored, by the way.'

'Wzappen?' Claire insisted.

Sophie told her that everything was okay; people had been arrested, nobody extra had died, the wake had been ruined, and so on. So Claire went back to sleep.

When she opened her eyes again, no time had passed, except that it definitely had. Claire could think quite clearly and her foot hurt quite a bit, and Sophie definitely wasn't on either side of her. She also desperately needed a wee. This was her main concern.

A solid, fleshy nurse with warm hands was taking her vitals. He smiled and told her that her temperature had gone down loads. He said it with such approval that Claire replied, 'Oh, thank you', as if she'd done it on purpose.

A young doctor came round and made eye contact almost exclusively with the file about her. He told her that her foot wasn't broken, just badly sprained, but she had also given herself flu and had almost killed herself by not eating or drinking and by gallivanting about the countryside digging up skeletons, which was very silly of her – although Claire was obviously the talk of the ward. Anyway, now that her fever was under control, she could go home with her friends and rest for a while and keep off that foot. But if she got bad again, she was to go straight back to hospital. Was that clear?

'Everything but the going-home bit,' said Claire. 'I live in London. That's ages away. How am I supposed to get back? Is there a train or something?'

'Well, I don't know about that. There are trains, but you'd have to look up the timetable. I was told that someone is filling out your forms at the ward desk and is taking you home. That's why you're being discharged.'

The curtains around Claire's bed were thrown violently apart. 'Hello, C!' cried Alex, a vision in a silver catsuit. The doctor beat a hasty retreat in the face of a hurricane that had ripped through a haberdasher's on its way to the hospital. At some point they had changed their hair from blue to bright pink. 'We're getting you out of here, *Cuckoo's Nest*-style!'

'You're going to throw a sink through a window and I'm going to be lobotomized?'

'Very funny. At what point does deliberate pedantry cease being a defence mechanism and start being you... being a dick? Here, eat this.' They thrust a hot sausage bap into Claire's hand. It was the most delicious thing she had ever eaten in her whole entire life.

'They look an extra from, like, a budget *Star Trek: TOS* cosplay group,' observed Sophie, strolling up behind them.

Alex had also brought Claire some clothes, since she had been admitted in a large men's-size cassock covered in mud, and possibly with trace particles of dead body – and, even if she'd wanted it back, the cassock had been taken as evidence. They waited while Claire went to the toilet and changed into a nice snuggly oversized jumper and leggings, and some fuzzy slipper-socks. She was also able to address the need for a wee, which made her feel less anxious about the world in general.

Basher was the one filling out her forms, it turned out. He smiled at Claire as Alex helped her over to the desk so that she could sign the paperwork.

'Come back, strange ghost-talking girl,' he murmured, giving her a brief hug. 'All is forgiven.'

'What he means is that *we* are very sorry and hope you forgive *us*,' said Alex, rolling their eyes.

They weren't given a wheelchair, but were allowed a hospital-issue crutch. Claire leaned heavily on it, but slightly more heavily on Basher, who was helping her. He felt strong but wiry, like he was made of Twiglets and muscle. Sophie noticed what she was doing and told Claire that she was a creep, but had probably earned it for now.

Alex was carrying her things – at least the ones that hadn't been impounded – along with the cassock (black) and dildo (purple). Claire was vaguely worried about the cassock. Was she going to be arrested for stealing it? Surely the police had bigger fish to fry than cassock-thieves? She also felt it was very important to explain to someone that the dildo was not in fact for personal use. This information needed to reach the CPS.

Unresisting, she was bundled into the front of Basher's car and covered in a blanket. Sophie sat behind her and kept leaning forward to check on her, like a family dog worried about the new baby. Alex slid into the back next to Sophie.

'Thanks for taking me home,' Claire said as they set off.

'We-e-e-ell,' said Alex, 'what else could we do? You clearly can't look after yourself. Not that Uncle B can, either, obviously.'

'Can too look after myself,' said Claire, snuggling into her blanket. Alex was pulling bits of embroidery out of their bag, and Basher was whistling tunelessly through his teeth. Alex started to explain the finer points of advanced embroidery techniques out loud for Sophie, pointing out how they formed different stitches to create different effects. It felt familiar. Claire promptly fell asleep again.

When Alex shook her awake, they were not in London. They were on the street outside the flat in Brighton. Claire voiced her confusion.

'What did you think we meant when we said "take you home"? You didn't think we'd leave you in that shithole flat, did you?' replied Alex, somewhat incredulously.

'In fairness, if we'd have gone back there you would have been found dead three weeks later, covered in bread-crumbs and fag ash,' said Soph.

Claire thought she would probably quit smoking. She was soon safely ensconced on the sofa, wrapped in a new layer of blanket, and had ibuprofen and Lucozade liberally administered. Basher put her foot up on a chair, on a cushion of frozen peas.

'You look like a cross between a mummified queen and a fat baby,' said Sophie. 'Actually, you know when Princess Margaret used to get wheeled around in a chair with big sunglasses on? That vibe.'

'I thought you were going to be nicer to me.'

'That is nicer, I said you look like a princess. It's a work in progress. Oh, all right. You did well, weirdo, and I'm glad you're not dead.'

Claire looked up and realized that Basher and Alex had, as best they could as a two-person group, gathered around her and were looking at her expectantly.

'G'wan then,' prompted Alex.

'What?'

'Come on, we all know you're dying to do a summing-up.'

'You even tried to do a summing-up while we were waiting for the ambulance at The Cloisters,' added Basher. 'I am afraid I did not appreciate how funny it was at the time.'

'Yeah, you tried to stand up and went, "I suppose you're wondering why I gathered you all here" and everything. Uncle B just went, "NO-O-O-O!" and you instantly passed out again. It was brilliant.'

'Oh,' said Claire. 'I don't remember any of that.' She was too tired to be embarrassed. Physically tired, not mentally. She was feeling quite awake and alert now, but if someone had demanded that she lift her arm an inch or they'd have to kill her, she'd have had to dictate her last will and testament.

Basher and Alex took turns explaining their side of the story. Alex had spotted Claire's ghastly visage peering through the pub windows, on account of the fact that she had done nothing to hide herself, but when they went to look, she'd already gone. Then later, when they heard that the rest of the family had hightailed it back to the house after the alarm had been tripped, Basher and Alex realized who must have tripped it. They had arrived just in time to restrain a distraught Clem, and to see Claire knock out Monty with a sex toy.

And they had also seen the ghosts. Only for a moment. A strange mist that, in one bright flash of lightning, looked for a second like a crowd of people. And then it was mist again, already thinning. Already never there. But it was enough.

'Pretty sure you're not a fraud any more, C,' said Alex, looking at their feet. 'Er, sorry again, about all of that.' They were uncharacteristically embarrassed. It made them sound like the rest of their family: posh and a bit stilted.

'I, too, am very sorry, and now believe in ghosts,' said Basher, nodding. 'Although *for the record*, not believing in ghosts would not make me the strange one.'

All of the rest of the Wellington-Forges – bar Figgy, who genuinely had no idea about any of it; Tuppence, who was likewise completely innocent and visibly relieved to see her soon-to-be ex-husband carted away; and Tristan, who had a broken nose and was under observation after hitting his head – were in custody in St Leonards police station. Bail was being arranged. Claire would need to be interviewed. It was, Basher said, probably a bit naughty of them to have spirited her away from the hospital without telling the police, and someone would be told off, but it would be him, so that was all right.

'So,' he said. 'The stage is yours. Let the summing-up commence.'

'Wait, though,' said Sophie. 'Are you two... all right?'

'Oh, fuck no, of course not,' said Basher, laughing. 'This is all awful. I also found out that Nana left me everything, but nobody told me, because they were planning to dispute it! Fabulous stuff.'

'He's been letting me smoke indoors and everything,' said Alex, lighting up as evidence. 'I am gravely concerned. Anyway. Off you go, Claire.'

'Oh. Right. Er.' She found that, having never actually done a murder summary before, she wasn't quite sure where to start. It looked easier on television. 'Right, so, it wasn't really murder. It was an accident. Michael told Kevin – Jerry, his real name was Jerry – about Arrowhead Beacon, a shell company that Monty and Hugh were using to embezzle funds from—'

'No, no, we know all that.' Basher cut her off, flapping a hand dismissively.

'Uncle T crumbled like a soggy biscuit as soon as a police officer, like, *looked* at him,' said Alex. 'Buckled

378

like a cheap belt. Tumbled like a badly-built Jenga tower. It was honestly a bit embarrassing.'

'I want to know how you figured it out,' said Bash. 'I didn't figure it out, and it was my job to figure things like that out. It is a point of some personal pride.'

'Well, a lot of it was luck really,' said Claire. She was trying to sound humble. The great detective. 'I spoke to Michael, see, about the accounts, and he told me he'd spoken to Kevin about it. So I started to think we might have got things mixed up. It wasn't really about what we *thought* it was about. Kevin got angry about something else, which is why we didn't see it, d'you see? It was the wrong... thingy. Motive. The motive didn't match the victim. Kevin accidentally stole Michael's motive.'

Claire realized she was not putting things very clearly.

'Ohmigod. Just lie about the order that you thought of stuff,' said Sophie. 'Go on. Say, "My first clue came when..."'

Claire smiled.

'Really,' she said, 'my first clue came when I found the blue notebook in your parents' office, but of course I didn't realize it at the time. But we'll come back to that. The second clue – of *vital* importance – was Basher hearing the boys arguing about breakfast. What he actually heard was Michael saying, "I'm serious about Beacon." Arrowhead Beacon! But the mind plays little tricks, and Basher thought he'd heard "bacon", and a year later all he could remember was that it was something about breakfast...'

She paused, and Alex went '*Ooooh*' in a very satisfactory way.

Claire explained how her conversation with Michael had started her thinking about Kevin's state of mind. He was already angry about how he'd been treated by the family, especially by Tristan and Monty, and now he had a way to pick a fight with them that wasn't about Figgy. And that, more importantly, gave him leverage.

That didn't prove that Kevin – or Jerry really, as she was trying to think of him now – was actually the victim. And she hadn't thought he was really, until she'd seen all the evil-eye charms in his room, and later had been looking at the picture of him on the plane and saw that he was holding something bright blue behind his boarding pass.

'And what do you hold alongside your boarding pass when you've just got on a plane?' she asked.

'Your passport!' exclaimed Basher.

'*Précisément*. I remembered seeing a blue notebook, the same bright blue with that evil-eye design on the cover, in the desk in the office at The Cloisters. I didn't realize it was a passport at first, because he had it in a protective passport cover, but when I saw all the evil-eye decorations in Jerry's bedroom I started to realize. I had to come back to the Cloisters to check, but I was pretty sure it wasn't a notebook by then. And if Jerry didn't have his passport...'

'He couldn't have left the country,' finished Basher.

'Exactly. From there, everything else started to make sense. Tristan and Jerry got into a shoving match, and

Jerry fell off the ha-ha and hit his head, and of course the first thing Tristan did was run to get his mum. That's what Tuppence and Alex heard in the kitchen – Tristan ruining his suit happened during the fight. Then Clem took control of the cover-up. She got the lads to carry Jerry inside, but upright. I was right about what The Clefs saw: not some brothers carrying one of their own inside, after a fight, but a family sneaking a body past them. They counted on the fact that The Clefs wouldn't have kept tabs on everyone there.'

And there was more.

'They stashed Jerry in the priest-hole for a day until they could bury him on Sunday night, and got Tristan away from you all, in case he broke down in front of you and Sami. That's why he went on the shoot with Hugh. And Sophie noticed that Tristan had two iPhones, when the company phones are Samsungs, so that second iPhone couldn't have been a company phone. Well, one of them was actually Jerry's. The messages that Figgy got were ones he tried to send on Saturday after the argument, but they only went through when Tristan and Monty left the area and the phone got a signal again. So they all arrived at exactly the same time.'

Later Tristan had used the phone to set up an Instagram account for Kevin, posting old photos that he found in the gallery. He, like the rest of the family, didn't know or could not remember Kevin's real name, and so he didn't find the Instagram that already existed under Jerry Maguire. But Claire did.

'How did you know it was Tris?' asked Basher.

'The *Kevin & Perry Go Large* references. He kept making them on the fake account. And he couldn't help it in real life, either.'

Alex raised a hand. 'Sorry to stop you mid-flow,' they said, 'but I have no idea what any of this means. Please remember I'm not old, like the rest of you.'

Claire snorted, then sneezed. '*Kevin & Perry Go Large* is a film, based on a sketch from a sketch-show, about two grown adults playing stereotypical teenagers. They go on a bender in Ibiza and try to have sex and become famous, that kind of thing. It came out when we were, like, ten or eleven, but people latched on to it. All that Eyeball Paul stuff – that you get more drunk if you do shots through your eyes. That was all around my school for years after.'

'I remember that,' said Soph. 'People stopped trying after a while, because it really stings. I bet Tristan was trying to use his initiative with the Instagram, because there's no way Clem or Monty is stupid enough to think that was a good idea. Like, the minute anyone went looking for Jerry, they'd be pinging his phone off whatever BT tower was next to Tristan.'

'Yeah, if Dad had known, he would have been furious, I bet,' said Alex. 'Poor old Uncle T.'

'Feels like we got lucky with the passport, too,' said Claire. 'Keeping that was a massive liability. I bet it fell out of Jerry's bag before they buried him, and then Clem found it and kept meaning to do something about it, but just shoved it in that drawer and half forgot about it. It was definitely Clementine who organized the cover-up, though. Moving the body, getting all her boys in line. She's... formidable.'

'One word for it!' snorted Soph.

'All right, so what about Alf and Grandad Hugh and the drug-smuggling?' asked Alex.

'Oh, that's easy, I can do that one,' broke in Soph. 'Hugh is a massive loser – no offence – and simply wants to fit in and be respected, like at the pheasant shoots. But he's a terrible shot – you told us that, Basher – and the only way he knows how to fix problems is with money. He was paying Alf to keep back pheasants that someone else shot and then pass them on to Hugh, to try and make it look like he bagged loads. I don't think he was fooling anyone. It was nothing to do with Mattie.'

'So the only thing that doesn't really fit is the crystal button,' said Basher, sounding almost wistful.

'I, er... I worked that one out too,' said Claire. She looked at Alex and was a bit shocked to see that they had started giggling.

'You *did*?' said Sophie in an incredulous tone.

Alex raised a hand like they were in class. 'I actually found out this one yesterday. Mum has left Dad. Not a moment too soon, as it turned out. I'm very pleased for her. But, um, as it happens, that is also the answer to the Mattie mystery, and the where-Mum-was-always-sneaking-off-to mystery. Because that is who Mum has left Dad for.'

'*Ohmigod. Amazing.*' Sophie looked positively thrilled.

'You mean...?' said Basher.

Alex rolled their eyes. 'Yes, panto cast-member, I mean that Mum and Mattie have done an elope. Well, half of one. Mattie has spent the last year setting herself up in a cottage in Cornwall for them both, partly using her ill-gotten Du Lotte Hotels gains. I'm told there is a herb garden, a collection of novelty teapots and two cats. Most middle-aged lesbian idyll ever.'

'And they share cardigans,' added Claire. 'I think the priest-hole was where they sometimes went for a secret daytime snog.'

Basher cracked his hands on his thighs. 'Well! Is that the wrap-up wrapped up then?' he said. 'Because life is going to get quite complicated, for a while.'

'Yeah, I suppose,' said Claire, suddenly gloomy again. 'It just all seems so... pointless. Michael said that when he told his boss, nobody cared about Arrowhead Beacon. There was no need for Monty to be scared, or for Tristan and Jerry to get into a fight. It was all for no reason.'

'It definitely was an accident, though?' asked Alex. 'I mean, the family name remains not a murderers' name?'

'Oh yes. Turns out Ted the gardener saw the whole thing,' said Claire.

'Making, basically, *all* of this pointless, if we'd only thought to ask him. LOL,' added Soph.

'I am *so* glad we are technically not murderers that I am not going to enquire about Ted the gardener,' commented Basher. 'Although I will be grappling with how absolutely cold-blooded my mum is, for a long time. You don't expect that, you know. She's... well, she's my *mum*. And I do not think the police believe it was an accident. There's going to be some kind of inquest, and it'll delay burying poor Kevin... Jerry. Possibly for months.'

'Well, from their point of view, I suppose that "Honestly, Officer, we've been hiding a body on our property for a year because of an accident, not a murder" isn't very convincing,' said Claire. 'Also, Monty did sort of try to do a light murder on me. A murderette.'

'A little bit of bodily harm, as a treat,' said Basher. 'In either case, I am choosing not to think too far into the future just at the moment. That's a problem for later. Come on, invalid. We should put you to bed. To be spoon-fed any soup other than chicken, and so on.' He bent over and actually picked Claire up, bride-over-the-threshold style. 'Oh, this was a foolhardy idea,' he murmured, almost instantly. 'Please get the doors, Nibling.'

Claire looked feebly at his peachy-fuzz jawline, because if she looked into his eyes she felt she might start crying. She caught the scent of sweet soap and clean laundry, and a little bit of sweat.

Basher carried her carefully, politely disguising the effort it took, down to his bedroom. The secret sanctum. It was airy, but smelled of paper. There were books stacked everywhere, in teetering piles up against the white walls. For some reason, Basher eschewed shelves. The double bed had been dressed in clean slate-blue sheets, like a wide, welcoming sea.

He turned his head down to look at her and smiled. Claire was struck by a sudden kind of madness. It was the knowledge that she had a future at all, that there would be people in it, that she was alive, and that Sophie was here and things would keep happening, one after the other. She flung her arms around Basher's neck and pressed her face towards his.

He went, 'Erk, what are you doing?' and reflexively dropped her.

Claire landed on the bed and bounced.

'Sorry! Sorry, are you all right? Oh dear. Sorry,' said Bash, looking guilty. 'Claire, I'm sorry, I'm gay. I assumed you knew!'

'Oh,' said Claire, going extremely red.

A million miles apart, but right next to each other, Alex and Sophie leaned against the wall and both laughed and laughed and laughed.

Epilogue

Weeks later there was another funeral, in a church that Sophie and Claire already knew. They stood a little apart from the other mourners, but Sue came up and said thank you for helping to find Jerry. She looked like her life was already over.

Sophie observed this with some curiosity, and asked Claire if she thought that was what her mum was like now, or if Sophie technically being missing allowed her to pretend things were going to be all right again. They talked about, maybe, going to visit her. One day. Eventually.

They loitered in the graveyard for a while after Jerry was buried, waiting for everyone else to leave. They stood by his graveside for a bit, but it stayed quiet. That made Claire happy.

Before they left, Claire put a clean cassock wrapped in brown paper by the door of the church. Then she went round the back of the building and took a brand-new football out of her bag. She looked around carefully, took out a knife and stabbed the football violently for several seconds.

'Cor!' said Luke, in disbelief, bouncing his new toy. 'Thanks!'

Sophie smiled. '*Ohmigod*, I really didn't think that was going to work,' she said. 'Trust you to murder a football, weirdo.'

'We've got to get going. Basher says he's having to physically restrain Alex from filling out the paperwork to start a kind of Mystery Inc., but for ghosts.'

'I think that's a good idea. You'd be brilliant at that. Anyway, Mystery Inc. for ghosts is just regular Mystery Inc.'

'No, it's not. The whole point of Mystery Inc. is that when they pull the sheet off the ghost, it's just a normal old man.'

'Ohmigod, why are you like this?'

So they went home. To Brighton.

Acknowledgements

Writing acknowledgements is immediately giving me anxiety because I'm going to forget someone. And, like, are they too long? How long are they supposed to be? Can you get acknowledgements *wrong...*?

I'll thank my family, *I guess,* particularly for leaving me alone when I was reading books I probably shouldn't have been at age 13.

Eternal and most important, thanks to Colm Ahern for being proud of every small piece of progress I ever made.

To Jay Wood: the burner of ships; bright-eyed; the first and most wonderful of readers.

Mega cheers to the other early readers: Chris Durston, Brendy Caldwell, Graham Smith, Hirun Cryer, Dean Rogers, Harry Scoble (also for being cool that I got a book published before him), and Johnny 'Rules' Chiodini, who didn't read but is generally lovely and supportive. To Chris Wallace for always texting me when I'm busy: fuck you pal x

Not many agents will put in the effort to help with edits and rewrites, and the intersection of those who will with those who provide lovely dog pictures is surely just Stevie Finegan at Zeno, a wonderful person who totally *gets it*.

Likewise, thank you to Sarah Hodgson at Atlantic and Anna Kaufman at PRH for being fabulous editors, especially to Sarah for looking after me at my first literary festival and Anna for often asking me to make bits sadder and, essentially, *make them kiss*.

Thank you so much to Felice McKeown, Kirsty Doole and Kate Straker for making me and my book both seem competent and cool and exciting – no mean feat, especially in the case of the 'me' bit. Thank you, too, to Hanna Kenne, Niccolò De Bianchi and Beth O'Rafferty for making sure this book physically exists, Ed Pickford for making it look like an actual book, and to Dave Woodhouse, Gemma Davis and Isabel Bogod for doing the tough bit of actually selling the thing.

A thank you and an apology to Art Director Richard Evans and my brilliant cover designer Lisa Horton, both for creating a cover that I love and putting up with me giving extremely vague vibes-based feedback, and then asking to move the broken window to a specific ground-floor window because it was very important to me for some reason.

Thank you Mandy Greenfield for the excellent copy-edit that caught how much I say 'actually', and putting up with me explaining, shame-facedly, when things are misspelled on purpose because I think it's funny. Thanks to Jan Adkins for proof reading at a time when I didn't think I had the strength to read this *again*.

I have nothing but pathetic gratitude to all the Irish writers who have immediately reached out and made me feel welcome.

Shout out to Coffee Cove, where almost all the edits on this book were finished with the help of vegetable soup, toasties, and massive scones.

Whoever it was who wrote an account of going to a WWE show and taking mushrooms on Reddit: it is one of my favourite pieces of writing and I think about you at least once a week.

And to any video game developers, writers, musicians, directors, artists and dream-weavers who ever made something I loved: thank you, thank you, thank you.

CLAIRE AND THE GANG WILL RETURN IN

DISPLEASURE ISLAND

COMING IN 2024